IT S
WITH WORDS . . .

Before I could see what was happening, he had me in a headlock. His hands were pressing tightly around my neck, digging into my skin. Then his hands tightened against my throat, making it difficult to breathe. It was all happening so quickly, I couldn't think. Suddenly, I was on the ground, my head hitting something very hard. I could see only a blur in front of me. Brian was pulling him off me.

"Get off him, you animal!" Brian was yelling. "You're overdoing it. You're supposed to scare him, not kill him!"

THE HATE CRIME

PHYLLIS KARAS

THE HATE CRIME is an original publication of Avon Books. This work has never before appeared in book form.

AVON BOOKS
A division of
The Hearst Corporation
1350 Avenue of the Americas
New York, New York 10019

Published by arrangement with the author
Library of Congress Catalog Card Number: 95-90103
ISBN: 0-380-78214-6
RL: 6.2

First Avon Flare Printing: October 1995

AVON FLARE TRADEMARK REG. U.S. PAT. OFF. AND IN OTHER COUNTRIES, MARCA REGISTRADA, HECHO EN U.S.A.

Printed in the U.S.A.

RA 10 9 8 7 6 5 4 3 2 1

To Belle Klasky and Toby Bondy,
best mother, best sister, best friends

With special thanks to Adam and Josh Karas,
sons, editors, and infinite sources of inspiration

1

I knew the minute I woke up that it was not going to be a good day. First of all, the sun was shining brightly, covering my whole face with its warmth. The last thing I wanted that day was good weather. The weather woman on the eleven o'clock news had promised rain and, stupidly, I had believed her. Good weather meant our lacrosse game against St. John's Prep would be played at 3:00 that afternoon. I would rather be grounded for a month than have to protect the net for Bromley High against St. John's Prep. We'd already played St. John's once this season. I'd made thirty-eight saves, but eighteen balls whizzed by me and we lost 18 to 5. Don't get me wrong. I love being a goalie, and, since I'm only a sophomore, I consider it an honor to be the starting varsity goalie for our team. And I don't fall apart every time we lose a game. But there's a difference between losing and being crushed, and St. John's always crushes us. Plus, Rachel was planning on going to the game. It would be the first game she ever saw me play, and the last thing I wanted was for her to see me blown out by the Prep.

Rachel Levy is the best looking girl in the sophomore class at Bromley High. She moved to Bromley from

New York last summer, and all the guys have been knocking themselves out trying to make a pass at her. How I got lucky enough to get her to notice me, I'll never know. But for the past three months we've been hanging out together, and I'm getting to feel more comfortable around her every time we're together.

The truth is, I've wanted a special girl for the past year. A lot of my friends have been hanging out with one girl. Sometimes it's a drag, but other times it's a lot of fun. I'm getting the idea it's something I'm ready for, too. If I have to be with a girl, Rachel seems like a good choice. Pam Rogers and I hung around together last summer, but my parents had a fit because she isn't Jewish. They kept saying it was my grandparents who were the most upset about my dating a Catholic girl, but since my grandparents live in Florida and never met Pam, I don't buy that. Most of the time, I get through to my mom about things, but this was one issue she and my father were sticking together on, and there was no budging her. Pam and I called it quits about six months ago, and I was a little bummed out. Until Rachel came into my life. It's not just that she's better looking than Pam, she's more fun to be around. And my parents are pumped over the fact that she's Jewish. But the thought of Rachel watching me come unglued by St. John's offense was enough to make me want to pull the covers back over my head.

Instead, I rolled out of bed and checked out the sky. Not a cloud to be seen. I barely had time to clear the sleep out of my brain before my mother was already on my case. "Up and at 'em!" she yelled outside my door. "It's one gorgeous day, Zack."

My mother is overly cheerful in the morning. She runs a shelter for stray dogs and cats and has to be there at 8:00 each morning, so she likes me and my ten-year-old brother Sam "up and at 'em" no later than

7:10. By the time she's getting us up, she's already jogged five miles and made us a nutritious breakfast. Sam, the little rat, is just like my mother. He's down there digging into the whole-wheat pancakes and freshly squeezed orange juice at one minute past seven. My dad's a lawyer—actually he's the district attorney for Essex County—and he's no morning person either. But he still manages to play tennis every morning at 7:00 before he heads to his office or the courtroom, so Mom kind of runs the morning show at our house. It's a "Wonder Years" rerun with her playing the blond mom and Sam handling the role of good-natured Kevin. I'm the obnoxious older brother, Wayne, who hits the kitchen with messy hair and half-closed eyes and irritates the mom till she runs out of patience and the sitcom turns nasty.

At 7:30, I was sitting at the kitchen table in my usual morning gloom, picking at my pancakes and listening to Sam talk about baseball practice, when my mother turned away from Sam and stared at me as if I were E.T., suddenly dropped in for a visit to earth. "Zack! Today's your big game against St. John's, isn't it?" she practically shrieked into my ear. "I almost forgot! I'm so glad the weather turned out great. Barbara's taking over the shelter for me so I can watch. It's at the Prep at three, isn't it?"

It wasn't bad enough that Rachel was going to watch me disintegrate in front of the St. John's defense. My mother, who never watches one of my games inconspicuously—never mind quietly or sanely—would be there too. "Yeah," I admitted, "but don't put yourself out to come. We're going to get killed."

"That's not what the *Item* said last night," she said. "They said your team had improved drastically since the last time you two teams met. Said Bromley was red hot, the team to watch. They cited you especially. I'm going to run upstairs and put on a red-and-black outfit." She leaned over to kiss my head, which is about the only part of my body I permit her to kiss these days. I didn't mean to be such a rat. I just can't help the way I feel about being kissed by my mother. It's . . . weird. "You just get out there and hold 'em back, tiger."

I groaned as she left the kitchen. I hate her red-and-black outfits. They're so noticeable. Just like the strays from the shelter she brings with her.

"You really gonna get massacred?" Sam asked as he ran his finger across his plate to scoop up the last of his maple syrup.

I handed him my plate. I had no appetite. "Not as massacred as I'm gonna massacre you if you don't shut up," I answered him. "I've got enough of a headache this morning from hearing you repeat every second of 'The Simpsons.' "

Sam shrugged his shoulders and dug into my breakfast. Almost nothing gets that kid riled up. To be truthful, I can never stay mad at him for more than a few seconds. He's only in sixth grade, but still, I've never seen him crack open a book. Yet he never brings home a grade lower than an A. In sixth grade, I had to work like a dog to get good grades, and they hadn't all been A's. Mom says Sam is gifted. Dad says he's a thirty-year-old midget. He also has the best arm in Bromley's Little League. It isn't easy having such a perfect little brother. Rachel thinks he's "absolutely adorable." She's sure I was every bit as cute four years ago.

"Keep your head down when they're coming at you," Sam said with a mouth full of my pancakes. "Last time you played the Prep, they scored on you every time you lifted your head."

I might have strangled the little kid with my bare hands, but I heard Ricky Berg honk his car's horn in our driveway, and I was out of there.

Rachel was waiting for me by my locker when I got to school. The girl was amazing. She had this long black hair that she wore in a giant braid. I had this fantasy that one day when the two of us were going at it pretty hot and heavy, she'd let me undo that braid and her hair would come falling down. That would be one unbelievable scene. "Hi, handsome," she said as she stood up on her tiptoes to give me a kiss. Rachel's real petite. I'm pretty tall, close to 5'10" and still growing, or so my uncle Phil, the doctor, always says, and hopefully he knows what he's talking about.

I like it when Rachel's so psyched to see me. "Hi there," I answered, returning her kiss. I meant to kiss her on her lips, but I have this tendency toward clumsiness, and I missed her lips and hit her chin.

She laughed. "Big game today, huh?" she asked as she fished one of her books out of my locker. She'd gotten in the habit of keeping some of her books in my locker. Her books had the same flowery smell she did. It was a bit much for a guy's locker, but I wasn't complaining. "I'm so glad it didn't rain the way they said it would."

I forced a smile. "Yeah. That sure was lucky."

"Hey." She looked up at me. "What's up? You sound funny."

"Nothing. Just nerves, I guess."

"One thing you don't have are nerves. I saw you before your last two games. Ice cubes don't come any cooler. And I've heard all about your goalie skills. What's going on here? Is it me? Does my coming make you nervous? 'Cause if it does, I won't go. No hard feelings. Just be honest with me."

Rachel had a thing about being honest. She had told me about her best friend in New York who used to tell these white lies. They weren't anything terrible, just exaggerations mostly and occasional omissions. But it got to the point where Rachel couldn't trust her. She said she never knew if her friend was giving her the real story or just bits and pieces of what really happened. It made her nuts. It sounded kind of weird to me, but I guess that must be the way girls think. I'd gotten the message. Lying was out with this girl. No problem. I wasn't much of a liar myself.

"Well, it's just that we're going to get our butts kicked by the Prep. It might not be a pretty scene. Next Wednesday, we play Rockville. We'll kill them. Maybe you should make that your first game."

Rachel gave me that serious look, the one that made her look school teacherish. It was different than her usual peppy look. "You're right, Zack. It really wouldn't be fair for me to come to watch you for the first time at a tough game against the Prep. You've got enough to worry about standing behind that net besides me on the sidelines watching your every move. I'm not coming." She smiled and squeezed my hand. "And I don't feel the least bit bad about it. You just get out there and do the best you can. And please keep your mask firmly covering that nose of yours. I did tell you how adorable your nose is, didn't I?"

I was feeling all hot and sweaty when Rachel took my hand. Rachel had incredible powers over me. It was as if she had a direct line to my hormone center. One signal from her and they were off and running. That little hand squeeze had gone straight through to my chief hormone. He'd released a spray of hormones which had flooded my sweat glands. It was only eight o'clock in the morning and I was already a hormonal mess. "You be there," I told Rachel. "If I get killed out there, I want your face to be the last one I see before I lose consciousness."

She squeezed my hand again and zipped up her book bag, staring at me with this silly grin. "If you're going under this soon in our relationship, buddy, you'll owe me a lot more than that before you flash out of here," she said, and I was beginning to think that her hormone control squad was in close contact with my guys.

Before I could say another word, she was gone, headed to her history class. I took a deep breath, made sure my shirt was covering my jeans zipper, and headed off to math. I knew that the Prep squad was going to murder me, but I sure was going to die one happy man.

•2

There is a certain feeling being behind the net that I've never been able to describe to anyone. Lots of the time, I'm bored to tears, just standing there, banging my lacrosse stick against the poles of the net, trying to keep myself centered and alert while the game is being played out at the other net. Other times, I'm a nervous wreck, watching the top attackman coming at me, moving his stick and the ball together in such perfect harmony there seems to be no way to separate the two until the ball finds a home inside the net or down my throat. But there are also those wonderful moments when I feel invincible, when my brain is at one with the ball and it's as if I can see the moves my opponent is going to make even before he imagines them. My body moves just where it should. Even through his helmet, I can see the surprised look on my opponent's face when I come out of the crease of the net to meet him, leaving the net totally empty, following his moves so perfectly it's as if now it is he and I who are one. When I'm hot, I'm hot. No one can get by me at those moments. No matter where he throws the ball, I'm there, snagging it away with my stick which has become a magnet for the ball, feeling like the greatest goalie on the face of the earth.

Well, that game against St. John's Prep was not one of my Superman days. I was more like Daffy Duck. I might as well have walked off the field and given my opponents an empty net. Oh, I had a few good moments. Maybe ten of them when I made ten good saves. But other than those fleeting moments of success, I was a dismal failure. My team tried not to get down on me. "Hang in there, buddy," Dana Kessel kept yelling at me.

"They're getting tired," Sean "Keldog" Kelly informed me after they'd scored their fifteenth goal.

"We're going to score back every one they get off you, man," Paul Edelman insisted when the score was 17 to 3. He did score our fourth goal a few seconds later, but the Prep followed it with two quick beauties in a row. If we'd had a backup goalie who was decent, Coach Wetherbee would have put him in, but Chip Norris was still having trouble with his ankle and the last thing Coach wanted was to hand him over as fodder to the Prep.

All during the game, I tried to ignore the crowd on the sidelines. But it was pretty hard to ignore my mom. If I even came close to getting a handle on the ball, she went nuts, shouting my name and every form of encouragement she could think of. When they scored off me, she yelled things like, "No sweat, Zack. Let 'em have one." Or, "Hang in there. That was just a lucky one." I don't know whether it was that my concentration was so bad or her voice was so loud, but there wasn't a word she shouted that I didn't hear.

And Rachel. She was standing just a few feet away from my mom. She had a spaz attack when I made a save and I even saw her and my mom hug during one of my rare good moments on the field. I also saw how close Ricky Berg was standing to her. It was sort of nice that my girlfriend and my best friend were getting along so great. Ricky had his own girlfriend, Patsy Ryan, but she was nowhere to be seen during the game. I'd never thought of myself as a jealous person, but I had to admit, even when I was under constant siege from the Prep team, that I was experiencing a fair blast of something close to jealousy. It was nice Rick liked Rachel and was being friendly to her. But did he have to touch her shoulder when he was telling her some probably ridiculous story?

In the last five minutes of the game, instead of putting in his weaker lines, the Prep coach kept his top men on the field. By then, the score was 26 to 7, and I was ready to throw up. I don't know what came over me, but when the advancing forward came at me, I didn't look at him. I just lowered my head and stared at the ball. Somehow, I rejected that ball. And the next eleven that came at me. We even scored three goals. A score of 26 to 10 was nothing to rave about, but you should have heard the way my team reacted in those last minutes. They went bonkers over my saves. I guess I can understand why: 37 to 7 would have been the worst humiliation possible. Twenty-six to ten against the Prep had a certain respectability about it. I could see Sam's face in the crowd. He was standing on the right side of the field with a couple of his sixth grade buddies. When the game ended, I threw him the game ball our coach had given me. I'd been thinking about giving it to Rachel, but I'd caught the way Sam had been looking at me during most of the game. He wasn't ashamed of his brother. Not then. Not ever, that I could remember.

I walked Rachel home after the game. I felt sweaty and gross, but that didn't seem to bother her. I caught the way she smiled at a group of her friends when we passed them. She was proud to be with me. I might have been the losing goalie, but in her eyes, I was a winner. It felt good to be with this pretty girl who liked me. If given a choice, I would have chosen to lose the game against the Prep and win Rachel.

"I love the way you run after that ball," Rachel said as we walked toward her house. "You're like a rabbit. You're as fast as the wind."

"Oh, yeah," I answered as nonchalantly as I could manage. "That's me. Big Chief Rabbit Who Runs with the Wind."

"No, I mean it." She punched my arm for emphasis. She was small, but I could see that her fist could do damage. "You are fast. But what I love the best is the way you come out of the net all the time. I was watching the other goalie. He's supposed to be the best in the league. Well, he looks petrified every time he comes away from the net. Like his life is in danger. But not you. You're dauntless."

I like the way Rachel uses big words. Luckily, I'm a pretty big reader so I know most of them. Plus, Mr. Braunstein keeps telling us it's good training for the SATs to use as many big words as you can. "Yeah, well, maybe, one of these days you'll even get to see me win a game."

Rachel gave me a few more good love taps. My arm was beginning to hurt. But I couldn't help smiling. It was hard to believe someone as little as Rachel could pack such a wallop. "Well, you better stop laughing at me," she said, "or else I'll come running up to your net during one of your games and distract you so badly, you won't know what's coming at you."

"Oh, yeah?" I swung her around and pulled her close to me so that the top of her head was level with my chin. Then I put my arms around her and kissed her on her forehead, right in the middle of the sidewalk. I'd never done that before. I would rather have gotten her lips, but the way she moved I was lucky to have gotten a shot at her forehead. "I'm shaking in my boots."

Rachel pulled away and giggled. Her face was red, but I could tell she liked the kiss.

A few minutes later, we were in front of her house. The Levys live in a real nice house. I've met them maybe four or five times and they've never been all that friendly to me. They are older than my parents, who are in their early forties. Mrs. Levy seemed nervous every time she saw me. Mr. Levy sort of acted like he'd just as soon not have me in his house. That bothered me since Pam's parents had never rejoiced either when I walked into their house.

When I mentioned all this to Rachel, she told me not to worry about it, that her parents were overprotective. "They treat everyone who comes into the house as if he's the enemy, out to rip me to shreds," she said. "Don't take it personally."

I tried to take her advice, but it did bother me that they didn't seem to like me, even though they didn't even know me well enough to dislike me. I kept thinking of the great "Seinfeld" episode where Jerry's mother is shocked that her son had an enemy and says, "But *everyone* likes Jerry." I could just imagine my mom saying something like that. And I could imagine Mr. and Mrs. Levy standing up and saying, "Well, we don't."

Rachel's father had moved from New York to Massachusetts because of his teaching job at Boston University. He had tenure, Rachel had explained to me, at Brooklyn College, which meant he could teach there forever, but B.U. sought him out for their religion department and made him chairman so he'd come to Boston. I doubt if he ever smiled. At least, not at me. He also looks like he had bad skin once. There are acne scars all over his face. Mrs. Levy is kind of chunky.

Rachel's an only child, and from what she told me, her mom never worked. Rachel never seemed all that comfortable talking about her parents, but I couldn't help being curious about them and why they seemed so unfriendly.

Mrs. Levy was busy getting supper ready when Rachel and I walked into the house. She looked down when she saw me, wiped her hands on her apron, and immediately brought a plate full of brownies over to me. I was surprised. That was the nicest thing she'd ever done for me. I knew she was a good cook. The house was always filled with great cooking smells, but this was the first time she'd offered me anything to eat. I was kind of embarrassed to be so sweaty and dirty, but she didn't seem to mind. She handed me a brownie which I ate immediately. It was still warm and delicious. Since my mom's idea of a good dessert is a carrot, I was especially grateful for the treat. "How was the baseball game, Zack?" she asked, as I polished off a second brownie. They were better than good.

"Lacrosse, Ma," Rachel said before I could get a word in. "I told you he's a lacrosse goalie a million times."

"Lacrosse, baseball—there's such a difference?" she asked. "They all have balls in them, don't they?"

Rachel looked like she was going to have a fit. She also didn't look the least bit interested in the brownies. "Ma, please, don't be so silly. Zack takes his game very seriously. He's a talented goalie. It's not a joke to him."

Mrs. Levy looked wounded. "Don't feel bad, Mrs. Levy," I said before Rachel could launch another attack at her mother. "My mother's not quite sure what I'm doing in the sport. All she knows is that someone throws a ball into my face, and if she's not at every game, I could get hurt."

Mrs. Levy shook her head worriedly. "It doesn't sound so nice to me," she said. She put the plate of brownies on the table in front of me and then turned around to take something out of the oven. "It sounds very dangerous."

"Gee," I said, "I was just joking . . . " Before I could say another word, Rachel was leading me out of the kitchen.

"Thanks for the brownies, Ma," she said. "I've got to study for my big French test now. Don't count on me for dinner."

Mrs. Levy kept her head aimed at the floor. I felt bad that I'd said something that might have upset her. I'd gone one step forward with her and three steps backward. I didn't have time to give it much more thought since Rachel's arm was propelling me out of the kitchen, directing my shoulders toward the direction of her bedroom, distracting me from any more thoughts about me and Mrs. Levy.

For the next half hour, Rachel and I sat on her bed, just kind of fooling around. I was sort of surprised that Mrs. Levy let us stay in Rachel's bedroom when she was home, but as long as Rachel said we were studying, she never objected. Mrs. Rogers never let us stay in Pam's bedroom when she was home, but luckily, she worked a lot, and Pam and I had plenty of time alone there. Rachel always left the door open, but Mrs. Levy never seemed to leave her kitchen when I was over.

Pam was my first real experience with "fooling around" with a girl. Mostly, we kissed, French kissing, too, and probably would have started heading toward second base if we'd lasted a little longer. Pam and I talked about a lot of different things in her bedroom, but her favorite subject was people. She seemed to know something about everybody in our class. And she could be real funny when she tore somebody apart. I always told her she could be a great talk show host, because she got down to the nitty-gritty about a person in ten seconds flat. After I told her that, she got real interested in the talk shows and it was hard to get her to stop watching them when I came over. Rachel was a lot like Pam in that she enjoyed kissing and hugging, but that was the farthest we'd gotten. One thing I liked about Rachel was that we didn't waste time watching television. We were getting real comfortable sitting beside each other on the bed, when Rachel suddenly pulled herself together, sat up straight, and ended that session. "Time to call it a day, Zack," she said as she straightened her sweater. "I've got a ton of work to do tonight."

It took me a little longer to pull my act together. I've always been impressed with how girls can snap out of these sessions so much quicker than guys. Parts of my body seem to have minds of their own and don't just flash back to normal in ten seconds. "I thought we were thinking of getting some work done ourselves," I said, trying make my voice sound normal, too.

"Cute," she said, using that little strong-arm tactic of hers to hoist me to my feet. "Only that kind of work isn't going to get me an A on my French test tomorrow."

"I know," I said as I made sure that my lacrosse shirt covered the front of my shorts. *"C'est temps pour moi partir, mon petite belle."*

"Ooh, I love it when you speak sexy French," she said as she escorted me out of her bedroom, offering me one last kiss.

I was walking out of the house when Mr. Levy came driving up the driveway. He was behind the wheel of his spiffy new red Camry. I love that car. He rolled down his window and waved at me as he headed into his garage. It wasn't a friendly wave or anything like that. But at least he didn't scowl at me the way he had the last time I'd seen him. Things were looking pretty good, I decided, as I slung my lacrosse stick and helmet and pads over my shoulder and headed home. Pretty darn good.

3

My father was there when I got home from the Levy's. It's pretty unusual for him to be home before seven o'clock. Since my dad's the district attorney, he gets to prosecute high-profile cases. Unfortunately, he brings all his work home with him, and they're never simple cases like shoplifting or traffic violations.

Last month, for instance, he prosecuted a sixteen-year-old boy from Lynnhurst, Danny Barkley, who murdered his fifteen-year-old girlfriend, Katie Sawyer. For the three months before they went to trial, that's all we heard about at dinner. How Danny was incorrigible, "a rotten apple," "a loaded gun." Danny pleaded not guilty, but my dad was able to get him prosecuted as an adult, and he ended up being found guilty of second-degree murder. Despite the fact that Danny was a real loser and never showed any sign of remorse, my dad still agonized about the case. If Danny's mother hadn't been so screwed up on drugs and his father hadn't abandoned the family ten years ago, Danny might not have ended up serving a fifteen-year sentence and a beautiful little cheerleader might not have landed on the bottom of a pond, weighted down with several pieces of iron around her ankles. Sometimes, I wish my father owned a restaurant or a store so we could sit at dinner and talk about roast beef or stereos. But my dad brings all his problems home and our dinner hours often end up making me depressed and nervous. How could anyone listen to stories about rape, murder, and armed robbery and enjoy his dinner?

"Heard you had a good game, Zack," my dad greeted me. He was in the kitchen making a salad. When he's involved in a murder case, he always starts cooking our meals. I don't know why. Maybe it makes him feel better. As much as I hate the discussion that goes along with his murder trials, I enjoy our meals a lot more when he's on one. My mom's a really lousy cook. Well, maybe not lousy, just real health conscious. One thing she's adamant about is no red meat at our table. Since she runs a shelter that promises never to put a cat or dog to sleep, it's kind of understandable, I guess.

"If you want to eat a dead cow," she always tells me when I start begging for a hamburger, "go order it in a restaurant. I'm in the business of saving animals, not cooking them."

My dad, however, has no such problem with dead animals. While he'd never go at it with my mother over a hamburger, he'll cook chicken in exotic ways. I looked at the pan he was putting into the oven. Hawaiian chicken. My favorite. His murder case had ended four days ago, but he was still cooking. And I wasn't complaining.

"Oh, yeah, a real great game," I answered. "Twenty-six to ten's a terrific score. Obviously, you spoke to Mom, not Wetherbee."

"Neither. I saw Gene Gorman from the *Item* at the court house. He had just come from covering your game. He said you were outstanding. He thinks you have the makings of a great college goalie."

"Yeah?" I was dying to play college lacrosse. Even though I was just a sophomore, I wanted to go to Duke. They were Division I in lacrosse, but I had two more seasons to perfect my skills. Like Browning said, "What's a heaven for, if not to improve your reach?" Well, he might not have said it exactly that way, but that was the general idea. I had to aim high. Luckily, I scored in the ninetieth percentile on my PSATs. "I wonder if he knows anybody at Duke."

"I don't know about that, but it's a good thing I'm clipping all his stories about your games. They'll look great with your applications."

I snagged a piece of pineapple out of the pan before he closed the oven door. "We play Rockville next Wednesday," I told him as he started to work on his Caesar salad. Caesar salad is the only salad he knows how to make, but he makes it good and garlicky. "I should have an easier time against them."

"I'd love to get to that one," he said. "Maybe if we recess early, I can make it over there for a half hour or so."

"Oh, are you on a new case?" I asked, wishing he wouldn't say yes but determined to handle this one better than the last. For some reason, I'd felt especially bad when Danny Barkley had been found guilty. I was proud that my father had built up such a strong case, and I really believed the kid was guilty, but he was only sixteen, and he was going to spend the next fifteen years behind bars. Sure, he deserved it, but it bothered me a lot. Plus, his going to jail wasn't going to bring his girlfriend back to life. My father always tries to explain to me that that isn't the point of justice being served—to make the victim come back to life—but it does provide solace of sorts for her loved ones and it does serve as a deterrent to future crime. I understand what he says, but I still feel lousy for the guilty party.

I sure hope that doesn't mean I have the heart of a criminal.

"Oh, yes," my dad answered me. "And this one I want to see over as quickly as possible."

He said that about all his cases. But I could sense he especially meant it about this one. "So, what's this one about?" I asked and took a deep breath. Maybe, if I was real lucky, it would be a simple breaking and entering. But rarely did my dad get the simple cases.

"It's a painful one, Zack." He closed the oven door and sat down at the kitchen table. I noticed that his hair looked grayer. I hate noticing that my parents look older. I try hard to ignore the fact that they're aging. Ever since my grandfather died after a heart attack two years ago, my grandmother has looked fragile to me. I hate to think about losing her the way we did my grandfather. If I have to start worrying about my father, too, I'll turn gray. "I don't have to tell you that this is all confidential."

My dad always says that before he tells me anything. I appreciate his confidence in my ability to keep a secret, but I usually see everything he tells me in the newspaper a day or so later. "I won't say a word to anyone," I promised.

"Okay. It's a hate crime. It'll be all over the news tonight. They discovered anti-Semitic graffiti on the door of Temple Israel in Rockville. It was pretty ugly stuff, Zack."

I have to be honest. I knew that was a terrible thing, but it didn't knock my socks off. After all, I'd been living with first-degree murder charges for the past month. Graffiti is terrible, but it's not murder. Still, I could see how upset my dad looked, so I tried to look the same way. "No kidding. That's gross. What did it say?"

"The usual. About Hitler not finishing the job with

the Holocaust, but there was something even worse this time.'' He hesitated for a minute before finishing. ''Most times, the anti-Semitic graffiti is the work of illiterates. Or at least people who don't know how to spell the names of the concentration camps correctly. But this time, whoever did it scribbled, actually pretty clearly, the names of seven concentration camps. And not all seven are that well known. And he drew a swastika next to each one.''

''Seven?'' I asked. ''Man, I didn't know there were that many camps.''

My dad gave me a disgusted look. ''You didn't?'' he asked. ''There were more than seven camps. There were concentration camps and labor camps and death camps. What exactly did they teach you in eight years of Hebrew school?''

''That two hours could go very, very slowly.''

''Come on, Zack. I'm serious. Did you learn anything except how to recite your Haftorah portion at your bar mitzvah?''

I was confused by my father's annoyance. We weren't a particularly religious family. I know my parents want me to marry a Jewish girl, but except for going to our temple three days a year for the high holidays, we don't practice our religion all that much. ''Not really, Dad. Mostly, I fooled around and got in trouble. But I saw *Schindler's List.* I know about the Holocaust. I'll read up about the camps in my Hebrew school books. I still have them.''

My dad smiled. ''Well, that's good. Anyhow, what makes all this so unsettling is that these vandals knew more than your average graffiti writer. I can't put my finger on it, but this particular hate crime sends shivers up my spine. I've put the case in a different category than the typical hate crime. Tell me something, Zack.

I'm curious. Do you know what constitutes a hate crime?''

I shook my head. ''I'm not real sure. But I guess, it's a crime caused by someone hating someone else.''

''More or less,'' he said. ''If you were to scribble 'John loves Jane' on someone's house, that would be vandalism. If someone were to scribble a swastika on our house, that would be a hate crime. That's threatening my life. Our office is pledged to be tough with any kind of hate crime in which a private citizen's rights are infringed upon. We've got to work closely with the police department on this one. There's been an alarming rash of anti-Semitic actions in the county over the past few years. There were four hundred and eighty hate crimes in our state alone last year. That's a lot, Zack. I was almost becoming immune to them. But this one really has me worried.''

My dad's attitude was making me nervous. He sounded like a get-tough D.A. But he also sounded like a worried Jew. ''It sounds pretty awful,'' I said. ''But you'll find out who did it and put him behind bars. 'Cracker Jack Jack' to the rescue.''

My dad tried to smile. But it wouldn't come. ''This is serious stuff, Zack. For all of us.''

''But your office has already started working on it, hasn't it?''

''Of course, we have. We've assigned a victim witness advocate, Sheryl Perlow, who will be the liaison officer between our office and the rabbi of Temple Israel and other rabbis in the area. Sheryl's top-notch at her job. And I intend to assure the clergy that we're going to find the perpetrator of the crime as soon as possible. I'm meeting with several rabbis early tomorrow morning to do just that. And . . . oh, that's enough. Thanks for hearing me out, Zack. Enough of my complaining and bringing all my depressing work home with me. Let's get this table set and this show on the road. I'm starved."

I was relieved to see my father get back to work on our dinner. It was hard to believe that after the murder case, this graffiti case was going to be such a tough one. Yet, the more I thought about it, the worse it seemed. Where had this person gotten this information? If he knew about concentration camps, how could he hate Jews? Maybe, he was one of those hidden Nazi criminals who hasn't ever been discovered and was hiding in our area. By the time my father had finished making the Caesar salad, I was actually feeling shivers up my spine, too.

When I was setting the table, Sam walked into the kitchen, holding a black-and-white cat. It had the most unbelievable green eyes I'd ever seen on a cat. And I've seen a lot of cats' eyes. "I'm afraid to ask where that came from," my father said, shaking his head as soon as he saw the cat.

"Mom said not to get attached to it," Sam said as he opened the refrigerator and took out the milk. "But it's a wicked smart cat."

"I'm sure it is," my father said. "Your mother only saves the lives of exceptionally brilliant animals, in case you guys didn't already know. Or maybe it's that the dumb ones never can figure out how to get to her shelter."

"Yeah, well, Mom found him and a white cat in a box on the front step of the shelter when she went in this morning," Sam said, stroking the cat's fur while it hungrily lapped up the milk. "There was a long letter inside the box from its owner. She said the cats were brothers and almost a year old. She loved both cats but she was homeless and sleeping in her car and was afraid they would freeze to death. She hated to give them up. She begged the shelter not to separate the cats but to find them a home together. Mom's trying, but she said it may take a while. She said she's getting more and more animals from homeless people these days. Barbara took the white cat home and Mom brought this one here. They named them Good and Plenty. This one's Good."

My father went over to pat the cat. I don't know why but this story depressed me as much as the graffiti. I wondered what the Levys were talking about during their dinner. Maybe the price of kosher hamburger. Or Rachel's French test. I'm sure it was a lot more appealing than what was being talked about in my kitchen.

Dinner was delicious, but the discussion was just about what I expected. Five minutes was dedicated to my lacrosse game, ten minutes to Sam's science project—something about hydraulic pumps that I couldn't even begin to follow—and the rest of the hour to hate crimes at Temple Israel and Good.

"You were quiet tonight," my mom remarked when I was helping her clear the table. My mom insists Sam and I help out with dinner. She sets up a schedule where either Sam or I am responsible for setting and clearing the dishes every night. Tonight was my night. "It can't be about the game. You were phenomenal."

"I'm okay," I said. "Just tired, I guess."

"Well, then, try and get a good night's sleep for a change."

"I will. I'm going to get some homework done now."

I was halfway out of the kitchen when she said, "Rachel's a lovely girl, Zack."

I couldn't get over how little my mom said about Rachel. Not that she'd said that much about Pam. It was mostly the way she looked when I said something about Pam. She'd smile and listen, but I knew she wasn't really hearing me. The only thing she wanted to hear me say was that Pam and I weren't a couple any longer. Oh, when Pam came over, my mom was polite to her. She'd ask her how her classes were going and invite her over for dinner sometimes. Pam thought my mom was cool and that she liked her. But she didn't know my mom. She didn't understand that my mom wasn't being herself with her.

Talk about being prejudiced. The only reason my parents didn't like Pam was because she wasn't Jewish. It was funny, but Pam's parents weren't any more crazy about me than my parents were about their daughter. Her father wasn't bad, but her mother never looked overjoyed when I came in. When I asked Pam about it, she said her mother was nasty to all her boyfriends, but I didn't believe that. I saw the way Mrs. Rogers acted toward Chris Calvani when I brought him over to Pam's once. Him, she smiled at. Sure, he's Catholic. I wouldn't have been surprised if Mrs. Rogers and my mother had gotten together and worked out this arrangement where they would each be real cold to the other's kid. Probably they're best friends now, my mom and Mrs. Rogers. They probably meet for lunch once a week, one week at the kosher deli in downtown Boston, and the other week at a little Irish restaurant, if such a type of restaurant exists, in South Boston.

Pam and I barely speak now, but our mothers might well be blood sisters. That was another depressing thing. I wish we could have ended our relationship as friends. But that didn't happen. It was more her than me. I tried to be friendly but she was ice every time she saw me. It was kind of a bummer that we couldn't be friends, but I guess that's just the way it is. I'm still not sure why we split. We just started arguing about little things and not having any fun together and before I knew what was happening, we were history. It wasn't even that one of us dumped the other. We just ended.

Kind of like a sitcom that stops being funny and no one watches it anymore. We just went off the air.

"Oh, thanks, Mom," I finally answered her, turning around to work on this conversation a bit more. I was happier talking about Rachel than about murderers and abandoned cats. "She thinks you're neat, too. Even if you do make a fool of yourself at my games."

"I can't help it, Zack. I try to control myself, but it's not easy to keep your mouth closed when your flesh and blood is being bombarded by an army of seven-foot animals, each one wielding a metal stick. Rachel got a little nervous a couple of times, too."

"Well, I guess you're both nuts over me and can't help it."

"Guess so."

I couldn't believe how little my mom had to say on this subject. It was like pulling teeth to get a compete sentence about Rachel out of her mouth. "You really think she's nuts about me?"

"Definitely."

"And that makes you happy?"

My mom stopped cleaning up the kitchen and looked at me. I recognized that look. She was weighing her words. It meant she was going to start a lecture of some sort. I didn't want that. "I mean, you like Rachel, don't you?" I asked, hoping for a simple answer and not a long drawn-out lecture about relationships between teenagers.

My mother shook her head. "Okay, Zack, let's stop pussyfooting around here. You want the truth? Here's the truth. It seems to be the kiss of death when I say something nice about your current girlfriend. On the other hand, if I don't like her, you hold on to her like she's Christie Brinkley. I'm afraid to open my mouth about this one. But since you don't seem to be willing to quit, here goes. I like her. Okay? She's smart and pretty and easy to talk to. She's even sweet to Sam when he answers the telephone. And, best of all, your mood has been upbeat since you started hanging around with her."

"And she's Jewish? Right."

"Right."

"And that's a big deal to you and Dad, right?"

"Right. And to Nana. Look, you're way too young to be involved in serious relationships now, but I just like you feeling comfortable around Jewish girls."

I was smiling. "Okay, I might as well tell you. We broke up after the game. She made some snide remark about my missing one goal and I let her have it. I was getting pretty sick of her, anyhow. She's too clingy. Besides, there's this new girl in my class, Maria Balzarini." The look on my mother's face was pure horror. I couldn't go on. "Okay. I surrender. I like Rachel. She's awesome. I've gotta study now."

My mom raced over and kissed me on the cheek. I hate it when she kisses me. I don't mean to sound cruel, but I just feel as if I shouldn't be kissing my mom all that much these days. A little peck on the top of my head or on my cheek is okay, I guess. But I hate it when she gets that hurt look on her face when I turn my face away. This time she got my cheek but good. She was smiling so much, I had to smile back. But I knew I had to be careful. I didn't want her to think she was in charge of my love life. It was nice she liked Rachel. But this was my business.

As I was heading up the stairs to tackle my homework, I started to think about the graffiti at the temple. It must have really been upsetting for anyone who lived through the Holocaust to have seen those names written beside swastikas. I suddenly remembered something I'd learned in Hebrew school about swastikas. One of my teachers had told us that because of the Nazis, a swastika was like a weapon. It meant you wanted to kill Jews. Who would do such a thing? Obviously, someone who hates Jews a lot and wants to kill them. Or maybe it was some Christian girl who liked a Jewish boy whose parents forced him to break up with her. Maybe it was Pam Rogers getting even with me. By the time I got to my room, I began to think I was cracking up. Pam would never do such a thing. She hadn't liked me that much. Besides, I had spent enough time thinking about the whole graffiti scene. After all, it hadn't been our temple. I had a lot of homework to do, but before I did any of that, I had to call Rachel. After all, I hadn't seen her in over two hours.

4

During the next week, Rachel and I saw each other every day. I won both my lacrosse games that she came to, and her team lost the two soccer games I saw. The truth is she isn't a good soccer player. She's too cautious, too worried about getting hurt to do well. But no matter how lousy her team is doing, she urges them on, cheering for all her teammates from the sidelines and hugging them like crazy whenever they do something good. It's funny, but I never thought about a girl's disposition that much until I got involved with Rachel. Pam could be real nice, but, man, could she be moody when something was bothering her. When things were going good between us, she'd send me cards almost every day. Funny cards and loving cards. And she'd write these real nice messages on them, telling me how I was her best friend in the whole world. I saved all her cards, and there must be a hundred of them. Sometimes, I read them over and it's hard to believe that someone liked me as much as she did.

But Rachel was different. She didn't write me sweet messages on cards. She just smiled when she saw me. And she had this weird way of knowing what I was thinking before I told her. Like once we were walking home from school and I got real hungry and before I said a thing, she made us stop at Friendly's and she bought me a huge sundae. You couldn't help liking this girl. At least I couldn't.

After our games and practices, we always went to her house to study. I tried to convince her to come to my house one day, but she said her mother preferred it when she came home. "Your mom works and that makes my mom nervous," she told me one afternoon in her room. "She's so old-fashioned, it's a joke. I mean, we could do anything we want in my bedroom even with the door open and she wouldn't know a thing, but she thinks I'm safe there." Rachel stopped and stared at me real hard. "Hey, your hair looks different today," she finally said. "Shorter. Did you get a haircut yesterday? Please don't cut it any shorter. I love your hair. If you changed your hair, like lost your curls, I just might break up with you."

Rachel was making me nervous. I have a real thing with my hair. A horrible fear of growing bald. My uncle Larry is bald. I mean, except for a little bit of hair around the back of his head, he is completely bald. His best friend always calls him the Eagle and my aunt Toby the Eaglette. I've seen the wedding pictures when he married my aunt. He had a complete head of hair then. Black curly hair, just like mine. I figured out that I had to be two when he married my aunt. But, from as far back as I can remember, he's always been bald. He told me it just happened overnight. One day he had hair and the next day he was bald. He jokes around a lot, but from what my mother has told me, that's pretty much what happened. To me, that seems like an unbelievable nightmare. Imagine going to bed with a full head of hair and waking up bald the next morning.

My mother tells me I'm nuts to worry about this. She says baldness is inherited from your mother, and her father died at age seventy-five with a full head of hair. Still, I do have this sensitivity about baldness, and hearing Rachel rave about my hair and say she'd break up with me if I went bald did not help my hair neurosis. "It was just a trim," I told her. "Maybe you better come to the barber with me next time to make sure it's cut the way you like it."

She looked surprised and happy. "I'd love that. I can't believe you'd really let me do that."

Now I wasn't so sure. I had a sudden image of walking into Wind and Waves with Rachel. Maybe my friends would think it was weird. It was hard to get this whole business straight of pleasing a girl and not making a fool of yourself around your friends. "Yeah, well, we'll see," I said. "I won't be needing a haircut for a while, anyhow. Actually, I usually don't cut my hair during lacrosse season. It's kind of a superstitious thing. Unless, of course, the whole team decides to shave their heads if we get into the championship or something."

Rachel turned white. "You'd never do that, would you?" she asked. "Oh, tell me you wouldn't do that, Zack. No matter what the rest of the team does, you wouldn't follow them blindly like that and shave your head, would you? I just couldn't bear it if you did."

The poor girl looked like she might faint. I was not happy with the way this whole conversation was going. The last thing I wanted to do that afternoon was get into a philosophical discussion about following the crowd. I just wanted to make out with Rachel. "I definitely wouldn't shave my head if it made you that upset," I said.

"You promise?" Rachel asked, still looking real weird.

"This hair is here to stay," I promised, forcing myself not to think about Uncle Larry. "Till the Red Sox win the World Series." She was still biting her lip. This shaved head stuff really did a number on her. "Okay. Forget it. Nothing, not even the Red Sox, will ever make me shave my head. Nothing." Luck was on my side. I'd said the perfect thing. The next thing I knew Rachel's face was back to normal and she was pushing me back down on the bed and kissing me. When Mrs. Levy's voice came from downstairs, calling Rachel's name, I wondered if the woman had some sort of X-ray vision. After all, the kitchen was underneath Rachel's bedroom. My luck, my girlfriend's mother was probably a relative of Superman. I watched silently as Rachel put herself back together and decided that it didn't matter if this girl's mother was Batgirl. I was hooked on this series.

5

Mrs. Levy was calling her daughter to ask me to stay for dinner that night. I was psyched. The smells were terrific. I knew it would be a great meal. Rachel wasn't so pleased. "I'm not so sure it's a good night," she told me when she repeated her mother's invitation. "Maybe you'll come another night."

"Whatever you want," I said. She had seemed all nervous when she returned to the bedroom to tell me what her mother had wanted. I figured it had something to do with her and her mother and I certainly wasn't going to push her to explain her feelings.

Pam had managed to tell me every secret in her life. In less than a month, I had learned that Pam's father was cranky and irritable for the first half hour he was home every evening, but a martini and two more during the evening transformed him into a pleasant human being. Pam worried that he was an alcoholic, but her mother refused to talk about it. I learned that Pam's mother had a mustache she bleached blond once a month and that she put mushrooms into every dish she cooked. I learned that Mrs. Rogers loved square dancing and Mr. Rogers wasn't crazy about it, but they went every Saturday night and had won some trophies. I learned that Pam was afraid of her parents divorcing, snakes, the dark, and getting fat and growing facial hair like her mother, aunts, and grandmother. She was jealous of her younger sister and hated her older brother who made her life miserable by hiding her underwear. And that's just the beginning.

It always made her mad that I couldn't come up with many secrets. I did tell her that my father's discussions about a lot of his cases depressed me and that my mother complained that my father's sister, Aunt Susan, was addicted to soap operas, but I couldn't come up with the quality of secrets Pam revealed. My family was, in comparison to hers, boring and dull. I was excited when I remembered that my mother's second cousin Billy, whom I'd never met, had spent three years in prison because he embezzled money from his mattress company. Pam liked that story and wanted more details, but my mother wasn't anxious to discuss the case whenever I brought it up. I don't think it's such a good thing to tell the person you like everything about yourself. A little secrecy is fine. If Rachel had a hang-up with her mother, I could wait forever to find out what it was.

That night, however, Rachel was able to overcome her hang-up enough to change her mind. "No, I think you should come tonight," she finally decided. "She'd be hurt if you refuse. Besides, the best thing my mother cooks is beef stew and tonight, you lucky dog, she's making it. Unfortunately, she's also prepared a potato kugel that's probably lumpy, but the stew is good enough to make up for that."

"Yes, but is she making Stove Top?" I joked.

"No way," Rachel answered. "It's not kosher."

"I was only joking," I tried to explain, but Rachel looked real serious.

"Well, are you staying or not?" she asked. "I mean, do you have to call your mom or what?"

"Since it's Tuesday, my mom will be working late at the shelter," I answered. "My dad's probably working late too since he's in court next week and Sam always eats at his best friend Andy's house on Tuesdays. His mom makes Stove Top."

This time Rachel smiled. "So, I'll tell my mother you're staying?"

"Yup. I'll call home and leave a message." As it turned out, Sam was home when I called. Andy had a bad cold. But he didn't mind eating alone. Sam's like that. Real independent. "Good and I will whip us up something tasty," he told me.

"Don't get too attached to that cat," I warned him. "Mom said she was close to getting him a permanent home."

"Don't worry," he said. "I'm used to having my serious relationships dissolved without any regard for my feelings."

I thought he was joking, but with Sam, it's hard to tell. He has a weird sense of humor. "Yeah, well, maybe you should switch your mouthwash," I said. Sam laughed and then hung up.

Mrs. Levy turned out to be a fantastic cook. Everything she served—the chicken soup, the beef stew, the kugel, the string beans with almonds, and the apple pie—was delicious. I'm so used to a mother who doesn't care about cooking that it was a treat to be fed by a woman who got pleasure from serving fantastic food. Every time I ate something, she watched to see if I liked it and when I remarked how good it was, her face lit up. "You're worth cooking for, Zack," she told me midway through dinner. "You have a wonderful appetite, but you're too thin. Rachel picks at her food. You eat."

Rachel shook her head. "If I eat too much, you tell me to watch myself," she said to her mother. She didn't say it meanly. Rachel seemed to get along just fine with her mother. The hang-up was nowhere to be seen. "If I eat too little, you ask what's wrong. When I figure out how to eat the way you like, I'll be ninety."

"So, tell me what classes you like in school," Mr. Levy asked when he was through eating his dinner. He was quiet when he was eating, but as soon as he finished his apple pie, he pushed his plate away and seemed to notice me for the first time. I was pretty sure he was as old as Mrs. Levy, but maybe because he was thinner, he seemed younger. I'm not good with adults' ages, but I'd guess these two were over fifty. "Rachel tells me you're a gifted student."

"Well, I'm not sure how gifted I am," I answered. "I've been in the talented and gifted class since third grade, but I'm the least gifted in that class. My younger brother, Sam, is really gifted. I'm just medium gifted."

Mr. Levy smiled. "I see there are all degrees of gifted in your family. But which classes do you enjoy the most in your program?"

"Literature," I said. "I like the Russian literature we're studying now."

Mr. Levy's smile faded. "Russian literature. What pieces of Russian literature are you studying now?"

I was not happy with the way this conversation was going. Suddenly, both Mrs. Levy and Rachel looked tense and Mr. Levy had stopped smiling. I enjoyed discussing literature in class with Mr. Braunstein. But Mr. Levy was a little scary. I took a deep breath and plunged in. "We read 'Misery' by Chekhov today. It's a painful story about a man whose son dies, but no one will listen to him talk about his grief."

Mr. Levy's face turned a little white, but there was still a small smile on his lips. "I know that story well," he said. "It's Chekhov at his finest. Tell me, Zack, was Iona's pain eased by the ending?"

"Oh, definitely," I said. I remembered Mr. Braunstein's words. " 'It's better to speak to an animal to release the grief inside of you than not to speak at all.' " I was quoting my teacher verbatim. " 'Humanity was too busy with its own problems to listen to Iona, but he found something willing to listen.' "

"And so he was helped?"

"A little. He still grieved over the loss of his son, but he'd begun the healing process."

Mr. Levy shook his head. "You're wrong, Zack," he said through pursed lips. "Very wrong. It's not good to speak of unspeakable pain. Unspeakable pain, by its own definition, cannot be spoken. Mankind is too busy to listen to stories of one man's pain. Chekhov wrote a beautifully crafted short story. One of his finest. But the moral of the story is not a sound one. Iona's pain was not to be healed. Not by the warmth of his mare's breath, nor by the ear of a compassionate human being."

"You are wrong, Isaac." Mrs. Levy was not looking at her husband as she spoke. She was staring at the dish in front of her, her eyes lowered toward the table. "It does help. It is far better than keeping the grief locked up inside of you where it will eat you up, slowly, bit by bit, day by day. But, sadly, some people cannot help themselves from allowing their grief to do just that."

I glanced at Rachel. She, too, was staring at her plate. Only she was biting her lower lip, as if she were struggling not to cry. I had no idea what was going on here, only this family had become as sad as Iona Potapov.

"Zack enjoyed reading *Macbeth*," Rachel said while I picked at my second slice of apple pie and wondered why on earth I had ever brought up the depressing *Misery*. "He really got into the witches' scenes."

Mr. Levy smiled again. "Ah, the witches." He sighed. " 'Fair is foul and foul is fair. When shall we three meet again? In thunder, lightning, or in rain? When the hurlyburly's done, when the battle's lost and won. Fair is foul, and foul is fair. Hover through the fog and filthy air.' "

He had a real rich voice. I'd always thought Mr. Braunstein had the best Shakespeare voice, but this guy had him beat. It must be something to have him as a teacher at B.U. I bet he made religion come alive, but good. For the next hour, the four of us sat there and took apart *Macbeth*. There wasn't one line of that play Mr. Levy didn't have imprinted on his brain. Rachel was really enjoying her father's performances, and Mrs. Levy didn't get up from her seat once to offer anybody more food during that hour. If Chekhov angered Mr. Levy, Shakespeare inspired him. And he inspired all three of us.

When he realized it was after ten, Mr. Levy suddenly ended our discussion. "We'll have to discuss Lady Macbeth's culpability in more detail at another time," he said as he stood up. "But I do have one last question for you, Zack. It has to do with your father." I saw the look Rachel gave him. It was not a happy look. "How is his investigation going concerning the graffiti at Temple Israel?" His voice was different now, no longer melodious but deadly serious. I hadn't realized what a relief it was to eat dinner and not discuss crime until Mr. Levy's question brought me back to reality. Even discussing the death of a loved one in Chekhov's short story or the murder of kings and noblemen's wives and children in *Macbeth* was better than talking about a murdered cheerleader. I was the son of a district attorney. Crime followed me like bees sought honey. A scarlet *C* might as well have been engraved on my chest.

Mrs. Levy spoke before I could answer. "Not now, Isaac," she said softly.

But Mr. Levy shook his head and continued his question. "I've been following it in the paper all week. I'm surprised there hasn't been an arrest yet. Are they close to one or not?"

"Daddy, that's not fair," Rachel said, again before I could speak. "Zack can't tell you anything that's not in the paper."

"I wish I could, Mr. Levy," I said. "But I honestly don't know any more than you know. I know my father's frustrated with the police investigation, but he doesn't feel they're doing anything wrong. It's just not moving along the way he hoped it would."

"What difference does it make if they find him?" Mr. Levy asked, almost to himself.

"It'll be a deterrent to others who try to commit the same type of hate crime," the son of the district attorney answered smartly.

"No, it won't," Mr. Levy insisted. "There will always be someone else out there who hates Jews so much that nothing will stop him from expressing that hate any way he can. Enough. Thank you for coming to dinner, Zack. And you're wrong about one thing. You are gifted. Very much so."

"I like your parents a lot," I told Rachel later that night on the telephone. "Your mom is the best cook. And I'd love to take a religion course with your father. What an orator. He must be a great teacher." I had some other questions I wanted to ask about her dad. Like did he always have such big mood swings and what did he have against Chekhov and exactly how old was he anyhow, but I restrained my curiosity.

"He is," she said. "I just hope he's happy at Boston

University. It's hard moving around in academia like this. Especially at his age. He's sixty-two, you know."

"Gee, he doesn't look it," I sort of lied, amazed that once again Rachel had been able to read my mind and answer a question I hadn't even asked. "But why did he decide to leave Brooklyn College and come here? I mean, it's the best thing that ever happened to me, but why did he do it?"

"He had his reasons," she said. "One was being made chairman of the religion department. The other was Elie Weisel."

Even I had heard of Elie Weisel, the famous Holocaust survivor who has written so much about the Holocaust and speaks so eloquently about it. "Do you actually know him?" I asked.

"Sure," she answered. "Maybe someday you can meet him here."

"That'd be awesome," I said.

"You're awesome," she said. And I believed her. When we hung up, I had the feeling that there was something else she wanted to tell me, but it would have to wait. That was cool. I'd learned a lot about Rachel and her parents for one night. There was a lot going on there that I couldn't even begin to fathom. Sometimes, I wondered if I thought too much like the son of a district attorney, always looking for clues and full of suspicions about people. The Levys were different. There was something going on below the surface. But why should I care? Rachel was beautiful and smart and nicc and totally above the surface. And her mom was the best cook I'd ever met.

•6

Rachel and I hung out with Ricky Berg and Patsy Ryan that Friday night. Patsy and Rachel aren't friends, but Rachel had no problem with the four of us hanging out together. However, she did make me promise we'd go to the party her best friend, Diane Halpert, was having the next weekend. Truthfully, I don't see what Ricky sees in Patsy. She's good-looking, but she can be real snobby. Her parents are wicked rich, and she's always telling everyone how she's going to prep school for her last two years of high school, as if Bromley High isn't good enough. Ricky says she's not that way when you get to know her. She sends money and letters to an orphan in Peru and volunteers at My Brother's Table. It's amazing she never talks about that, but brags constantly about her trips and possessions. Ricky says she's nervous around me and wants to impress me. That makes as much sense as her not admitting she can be a good person. Sometimes I give up trying to understand girls. Anyhow, that night, we went to Rinaldo's for pizza and then to Revere to see *Forget Paris*.

Patsy spent most of our time in Rinaldo's describing her parents' new condo in Palm Beach. They also have one in Lake Tahoe, which apparently is the hottest place for all the celebrities to ski, but the Florida condo is their newest baby. "It has tons of bathrooms and a fabulous view of the ocean," she told us over and over. "You guys have got to come see it. Or maybe you'd have a better time in Lake Tahoe."

"Ooh, that would be fun," Rachel said. "Even if I don't know how to put on a pair of skis."

"Oh, you're athletic," Patsy said. "You'd learn in no time. And I have the perfect ski outfit for you. It's the same shade of blue as your eyes. I can't wait for you all to come."

"Zack will have to teach me how to ski in Vermont first," Rachel said.

"We'll plan a ski weekend up there for the four of us next year as soon as the snow falls," Patsy said. "Wouldn't that be a ball? Zack can teach us all how to use a monoski. I'll never forget how great you were on that thing when we took that class trip to Loon last year, Zack. I'll get my parents to give us some frequent flyer coupons. Doesn't it sound like a great idea, Ricky?"

"Sure does," Ricky said which really amazed me since skiing was definitely not Ricky's idea of a good time. He'd gone skiing in New Hampshire with my family a couple of times but spent most of the time facedown in the snow. Skating, he did incredibly, but skiing, no way. Amazing how Patsy could get him to do things. Patsy and Rachel and me, that is.

"But the best part of the whole condo is that my parents will be going two weekends a month." Patsy had left Tahoe and was back in Palm Beach.

"You'll have a great tan all next winter," Rachel said. She was a great listener. No matter how Patsy went on, Rachel acted like she cared what Patsy was saying. I doubted that Rachel was interested in rugs and bed quilts, but she sure asked enough questions to convince Patsy she was impressed with the Ryans' home furnishings. It was great when she'd squeeze my hand to show me where her interest really belonged. Even Ricky seemed to be having a tough time listening to Patsy's bragging. "No reason for you to go to Tan-a-Rama with us poor pale folks," Rachel said when Patsy took a few bites of her pizza and gave the three of us a five-minute break.

Patsy put down her pizza and stared at Rachel as if she'd lost her marbles. "I'm not going to Florida," she informed us. "The great part of the whole scene is that I'll be on my own two weekends a month all winter. That's why they're sending me to prep school. So they don't have to worry about me while they're gone. Well, believe me, I'll be home those weekends. Home alone in Bromley." She squeezed Ricky's hand for emphasis. "Won't that be awesome?"

Ricky shook his head in agreement. Ricky's the strong silent type. It takes a lot to get him excited. His parents are divorced and he's not all that nuts over his stepfather. His mom's been married to Roger since Ricky was two years old, so you'd think Ricky would treat him like a real father. Especially since his real father lives in California and doesn't exactly kill himself to see Ricky. Roger's a real funny guy who likes to have us kids over. He'll cook us omelets or make a pizza and he tells great jokes. But Ricky's always nervous around his stepfather. It's like he can't wait for Roger to leave. Roger usually takes the hint and takes off. I've tried to talk to Ricky about what's going on between him and his stepfather, but he never wants to discuss it. All he says about Roger is "He's not so funny when you have to live with him." My parents have hung out with Ricky's mom and Roger, and my mom says Roger's a great guy. She says Ricky won't give him a chance.

Anyhow, Ricky and I have been best friends forever, but we're real opposites. Like in sports. Ricky's sport is tennis. He likes doubles. He claims that way you never have to worry if you're having a bad day. If so, your partner can work harder for you. He thinks I'm nuts to be a lacrosse goalie. "I could never stand having all those players coming at me and have to take the responsibility of screwing up once and losing a game," he told me. "It's too high-pressure for me."

I knew his relationship with Patsy wouldn't make it through the summer. He'll never be happy with a girl who goes to prep school and only comes home on weekends. He has to have a steady girlfriend. I knew he and Patsy would be history by the end of July. I wouldn't have minded if she took off by Memorial Day. I felt bad I made her nervous, but that girl just didn't do a thing for me.

"Sounds great," he said to Patsy. She kissed his ear in response.

Rachel took her third piece of the cheese and mushroom pizza we were sharing and started to bite it around the edges. It's kind of funny the way she eats pizza. Sort of like a rabbit, teeth first, saving the center for the last, always using her napkin to clean around her mouth. Patsy, on the other hand, attacks her food like she hasn't eaten in weeks and, despite her big bucks, has never been told what a napkin is used for. Patsy and Ricky were working on a pepperoni and sausage pizza, my ultimate favorite, but a no-go for kosher Rachel. "Are you worried about starting a new school next year?" she asked Patsy when Patsy finished describing the Jacuzzi in the Palm Beach condo.

"Not really," Patsy answered. "I mean, I already know my roommate. She's my father's business partner's daughter. And I know a lot of kids there. I've gone up a couple of times this year. And I even know the tennis coach. It's not gonna be such a big deal."

"It must have been hard for you to move to a new town this year," Ricky said, looking at Rachel. "Moving from New York to Bromley must be like stepping backward about a hundred years in time."

Rachel laughed. "Not really. I lived in a pretty quiet section of Brooklyn. And the school I went to was smaller than Bromley High."

"It was a Hebrew day school," I said, in case anyone was curious. Patsy's eyes opened wide on that one. Ricky was Jewish, but Patsy wasn't, a fact that didn't seem to bother Ricky's mom as much as Pam's Catholicism had shaken up my parents. Mrs. Berg managed to be a lot nicer to Patsy than my mother'd been to Pam. "Rachel's pretty fluent in Hebrew," I told Patsy.

"Wow," Patsy said. "That's neat. My parents said lots of their neighbors in Palm Beach are Jewish. And very rich."

"I bet," Ricky said. Then he turned back to Rachel. "It's funny, but I don't think of you as religious. I mean, I know you're observant, like with the kosher food and all, but you just don't seem that kind to me."

"What kind is that?" Rachel was smiling.

"Oh, I don't know," Ricky said. "I guess, like Freda Kaufman. She goes to Maimonides in Boston and covers her head and wears long black dresses."

"My mother wanted me to go to Maimonides," Rachel said, "but my father and I convinced her it would be too big a commute for me. Besides, he was impressed with what a good school Bromley is. I've met Freda a couple of times and I like her. I cover my head, too."

This time I was surprised. "You do?" I asked. "I've never seen you wear a kerchief like Freda."

"I wear a ribbon in my braid. It's my thing. My mother wears a wig."

"She does?" I couldn't believe it. Mrs. Levy's hair looked real, nothing fancy, just normal hair. "I didn't realize that."

"Sounds like there's a lot of things about this girl you don't know," Ricky said, and for a second I thought about punching out his lights.

But Rachel put down her pizza and kissed me on the cheek. "Oh, he knows everything that's important," she said with enough sexiness to shut up my supposed best friend.

Later that evening, Rachel and I went back to her house and saw *Indecent Proposal* on cable. The movie wasn't great but Demi Moore is hot and Woody Harrelson is cool.

"I can't believe that any guy would give his wife to another man like that," I said after the movie ended, my arms wrapped around Rachel. "No one could pay me enough money to give you to him for a night."

"Oh, come on," she teased. "You wouldn't be tempted for a million dollars?"

"Absolutely not. Maybe with another wife, but not with you."

"I'm so flattered."

"Why, would you give me to some other woman for a night for a million dollars?"

Rachel took a long time to answer that one. She moved to the side to face me. "You want me to be truthful?"

"Sure."

"Well, if we desperately needed the money for something, like to pay off a big debt or for some huge medical bills, I might sacrifice you. I wouldn't be happy about it, but if I absolutely had to do it for the money, like to save one of our children, I would do it."

"You're real generous with my body," I said. "But what if the person wanted yours? Would you do it?"

"Oh, that's so much harder. I'd hate to be unfaithful to you. But, again, if it were a matter of life and death, I'd sacrifice my own body."

"Well, I wouldn't let you. I'd figure out some other way to get the money. Once we're man and wife, I'm the only guy who's going to have your body, three hundred and sixty-five days a year. That's the way nice Jewish couples live once they're married."

"Not all nice Jewish couples," Rachel said. "Orthodox couples don't sleep together during the two weeks when the wife is unclean."

I wasn't all that comfortable with that "unclean" stuff. "Your parents aren't that orthodox, are they?" I asked, hoping to change the subject a little.

"No," she answered. "They keep kosher because my mother insists on it. And my mother wears a wig. But that's all they do. I know it sounds kind of weird, but that's how they operate. Still, I've always been kind of fascinated with the Orthodox way of Judaism. I feel it's only fair to tell you that now. Before you get seriously involved with me, that is."

I couldn't tell if she was joking. I kept looking at her face for a smile, but I couldn't find one. She was dead serious. "This is pretty heavy stuff, Rachel. Remember who you're talking to. The king of the cheeseburgers and pork lo mein. I'm willing to give that up, but two weeks a month—no way!"

"Then you'll have to marry someone else."

For a few minutes, the two of us sat there in silence. Rachel finally broke the silence. "This is ridiculous," she said. "We've been dating three and a half months. God only knows what's going to happen between us during the next ten years. I could become a Buddhist and you could become an Orthodox Jew. Now, could we please just enjoy the present?''

''Absolutely,'' I agreed and pulled her closer. Slowly, I began to unbraid her hair. Rachel and I made it to second base that night. With her ribbon lying on the floor beside me, I felt as if I were the general of a victorious army. My troops and I had seized control of the citadel and the view from the top of the hill was spectacular.

7

Saturday, Rachel came with me to my mom's animal shelter. I try to help out my mom two Saturdays a month. That's the busiest day of the week for her, the day prospective owners come to look over the dogs and cats. I enjoy hanging out there. My mom's had this shelter for about ten years and she's never once had to put an animal to sleep. She always manages to find a home for the dog or cat. Sometimes, she uses foster homes, people who will take care of the animal for a month or so until she finds it a permanent home, but somehow or other, things always work out fine. A lot of newspapers have written articles about my mom and her shelter. And they all say that my mom's the reason the shelter is so successful. She doesn't stop until she finds the right home for each animal. And she's fussy. Not just anybody gets to take one of her animals home. Everybody wanting a pet has to fill out a long questionnaire and be interviewed by my mom or one of her staff before they get the animal. Lots of times, my mother makes a surprise house visit and checks out the prospective owner's house to make sure it's the right house and family for each pet.

Rachel was pretty excited about working in the shelter with me. "I'd do anything for one of those dogs," she told me on our way over to the shelter, "but my mother just won't have one. She says my father's allergic to dogs and cats. I think she's making that up to shut me up."

"Some dogs have hair instead of fur," I told her. "They're supposed to be perfect for people with allergies. Why don't you tell her about a Lhasa apso or a bichon frise?"

"My God," she said, "how do they come up with names like those? Beagle or boxer sounds fine, but bichon frise? Give me a break."

Rachel looked pretty that morning. Ricky had mentioned the dimples in her cheeks earlier that morning when he'd called to see if I was going to the shelter. I'd never noticed them before. "Rachel has the most gorgeous dimples I've ever seen on a chick," he'd told me. "The only dimple Patsy has is her mouth which you could mistake for Hoover Dam. She's really getting on my nerves lately."

He was dying to come to the shelter with me and Rachel, but I hadn't asked him. I knew I was being rude since he always came with me on Saturdays, but I felt like having Rachel to myself. I knew my mother would be thrilled to see her. And she was. She was also so busy she looked ready to collapse when we walked into the shelter a few minutes before ten. "Thank heavens, you're both here," she said as soon as she saw us. "I've never had a morning like this. They were lined up outside the shelter when I got here at eight. I've never seen so many people wanting to adopt. It must be the weather. Spring always draws in new dog owners. But never like this. And we found four new puppies on our doorstep this morning in a beautiful little basket. Aren't they precious? But they can't be more than three weeks old. They need to be bottle fed. How 'bout you two helping out with the puppies for a little bit so I can give Barbara a hand with the interviews?''

''Oh, we'd love to,'' Rachel said. ''I just love this place, Mrs. Stone. It's so warm and cozy. No wonder everyone says it's the best shelter anywhere.''

That was it. For the first time ever, my mom was speechless. Smiling broadly, she put her arm around Rachel and led the two of us over to the back room where the four little puppies were huddled in their basket. For the next three hours, Rachel and I sat cross-legged on the floor, bottle-feeding the little black-and-white puppies. Each one fit into the palm of my hand. Rachel was out of her mind. But she took her job seriously, making certain the bottle was aimed into the puppy's mouth, and singing songs as she rocked and fed each one.

My mom came in several times to check on our progress. ''You're a natural little mother,'' she told Rachel, and Rachel beamed.

''I'd love to take one of those babies home,'' she told my mother, ''but my father's allergic.''

''Well, you come in anytime you want and help out,'' my mom said.

''I'd love to,'' Rachel said.

''Has anyone noticed how terrific I am with these guys?'' I asked. Just then, the guy I was feeding urinated all over my shirt. It was hard to believe that something so small had so much urine in his body. This guy had a half-gallon tank. To my mother and Rachel, this was the funniest thing they'd ever seen. I didn't think they were ever going to stop laughing. ''Very funny,'' I muttered as I stood up to get some paper towels for myself since no one was going to help me. But I wasn't mad. Sure I was wet, but I couldn't remember ever feeling so good.

* * *

Mrs. Levy was baking some cookies when we returned to Rachel's house later that afternoon. She seemed happy to see me. "So, tell me," she said while she poured me some milk and filled a plate with warm chocolate chip cookies, "did you sell a lot of dogs today at Zack's mother's store?"

"I told you, Ma, that's not what Mrs. Stone does," Rachel said. "It's not a pet store. It's an animal shelter. Zack's mother takes in dogs and cats that no one else wants and finds them homes. She promises never to put them to sleep."

"This is a business she runs?" Mrs Levy looked confused.

"Sort of," I told her. "You see, she charges the people who come to adopt the dogs and cats. It's not as much as they would pay for a dog or cat in a real pet store, but it's enough to help cover her expenses. She has all the animals neutered before she sells them to the new owners. That's a big expense. But she has an arrangement with a local vet, so that keeps the costs down. She sends out a monthly newsletter to all her owners and dog lovers, and lots of her readers send in contributions. My dad says it's a miracle she meets her monthly expenses, but she always does."

"She's amazing, your mother," Rachel said. "I can't believe how hard she works at that shelter. She's everywhere. And the way she checks out the new owners—like she's the head of an adoption agency giving out babies. I really admire her."

"Well, she's great with animals," I said, smiling at Mrs. Levy who looked overwhelmed by her daughter's enthusiasm for my mother. "But she has never baked chocolate chip cookies like these. What's in these cookies, Mrs. Levy?"

"Oh, don't be silly," Mrs Levy said, brightening. "They're nothing special."

Rachel shook her head. "Are you kidding?" she said. "Nothing special? I wouldn't say that. My mother grates chocolate and oatmeal into these babies, so they're nutritious as well as delicious. It's her own recipe. I keep telling her she should submit it to the Pillsbury Bake-off."

Now Mrs. Levy was blushing. "I wish you could teach my mother to bake like this," I said. "Did your mother teach you to bake when you were little?"

Mrs. Levy's blush disappeared. And Rachel turned pale, too. "I mean, I thought I detected a slight accent in your voice, Mrs. Levy," I said. "Were you born in Europe? One of my grandmother's closest friends was born in Germany. Elsa Goodman. She's a baker herself. She made my parents' wedding cake. Everyone says that a wedding without one of Elsa's cakes is not a real wedding." Instead of dispelling the gloom, my words were adding to it. But I couldn't shut up. No matter how hard I tried to keep quiet, my tongue just kept wagging. "Actually, Elsa and her husband, Herbert, were both born in Germany. They came to this country when they were young. They have two daughters. They're good friends of my mother. One writes cookbooks. Karen Madorsky is her married name."

Rachel rescued me. "I bought you one of her cookbooks, Ma," she said. "Remember? Last Chanukah. It wasn't a kosher cookbook, but it had some kosher recipes. You got that recipe for cranberry-spinach-meatloaf from it."

Mrs. Levy shook her head slowly. The color was coming back. "Oh, yes," she said. "It was a lovely book. I found some wonderful recipes in it."

"I could get her to autograph it if you'd like," I said. "She visits my mom a lot."

"That would be fine," Mrs. Levy said. "But if you would excuse me for a minute, I need to do something upstairs.'' Before she left the kitchen, she smiled at me. Rachel put her arms around her mother and hugged her.

The minute her mother was out of the room, Rachel leaned across the kitchen table and squeezed my hand. ''Don't feel bad, Zack,'' she said. ''You had no way of knowing. My mother has some sad memories about her life in Germany. Still, it's good for her to talk about it. Please don't worry about it.''

Rachel was looking at me so warmly I could not resist. I stood up and pulled her face toward me, kissing her for as long as I could before I began to lose my balance from my position leaning across the table from her. My hand shattered a couple of chocolate chip oatmeal cookies as it came down on the table. But that didn't matter. Nothing, certainly not a few broken cookies, could spoil this perfect day for me.

8

There was a break in the graffiti case on Sunday morning. My dad was out jogging with my mom when the call came from his office. It sounded urgent so I got on my bike and tracked them down. My dad spent the rest of the day in his office with the Rockville police. When he got home, it was nearly midnight, but I was up, reading *Death of a Salesman* for a test on Monday.

My father was totally revved up. Sam was sleeping, but my mom and I came downstairs and sat in the kitchen, eating frozen yogurt and cut-up fruit, while my father went over all the new information on his case.

The police had made an arrest that morning. They had arrested a fifteen-year-old boy from Rockville named Brian Murphy. His handwriting matched the graffiti. The police had gotten his name from an anonymous phone call late Saturday night. He was going to be arraigned in Rockville District Court at nine o'clock on Monday morning. Brian came from a respected Rockville family. He'd never been in trouble with the law before. He was a top student at Rockville High. I knew the name the minute my father mentioned it. He was the leading scorer for the Rockville lacrosse team.

We'd even gone to the same lacrosse summer camp the past summer. The camp lasted for five days, and we'd been on the same team a couple of times. We hadn't had that much to do with each other since it was just a day camp, but we played games and received instructions from area coaches all day long. Still, from what I'd seen of him, he seemed like an okay kid. Last season, we'd talked a little after the Bromley-Rockville game. He told me I'd robbed him of a couple of great goals. And I told him he'd taken a year off my life with each one of his nasty shots.

"It doesn't make any sense," my father kept saying as he spooned Ben and Jerry's Heath Bar Crunch frozen yogurt into his mouth. "This is not the typical hate crime perpetrator. His parents are law-abiding people. They belong to a church. His father's a dentist. His mother's a nursery school teacher. She's in a state of shock."

"Has he confessed?" I asked. I simply couldn't imagine Brian Murphy going to jail.

"He kept saying, 'I don't understand what's going on.' I'm sure he'll plead not guilty."

"Is he in jail right now?" I asked.

"No," my father answered. "His lawyer posted bail. He's home with his parents. This whole case has me baffled."

"What does Patty say?" my mother asked. Patty was my father's most important assistant. Whenever my mother needed to make sure my father was somewhere important, she'd tell Patty about it. Patty made sure my father got home in time for birthdays, weddings, or anniversaries. My father said she was the smartest person in his office.

"Patty's as confused as me," my father said. "She agrees this kid doesn't have the profile of a hate crime perpetrator. He has the face of a choirboy. He was having a hard time fighting back tears at the police station.

But we'll get to the bottom of it. It's just going to take some time."

"You know, this really is scary," my mom said, putting down her spoon. "I mean, if it were a scummy little kid from an abusive home with a long history of breaking the law, I'd feel a lot better about the whole thing. But Brian Murphy sounds like Mr. Teenage America. What would make a kid like that go out and commit such a terribly offensive act? It frightens me, Jack."

"I agree," my father said. "When nice Americans start committing hate crimes, we're in big trouble. Patty was going over the results of a new study of hate crimes in the Boston area. The researchers concluded that fifty-eight percent of all hate crimes are committed for the thrill of it. Imagine that. Just because it's fun. They found that the most likely targets for hate crimes today are Asians and Latinos, followed by homosexuals, blacks, and Jews. Though they only focused on a single eighteen-month period when three hundred fifty-nine hate crimes were committed, they concluded the incidence of such crimes is on the rise. I'm telling you, we're in for a big increase in hate crimes. Children of baby boomers are reaching their teenage years, the prime years for committing hate crimes. It's pretty scary that these thrill seekers didn't even know their victims and appeared to have no single racial focus. If a member of one victim group is not available, then another will do. They go out looking for a black, but they find a Latino first and he will do just fine. So they beat him up and go home feeling like they've had a great night. These hate crimes are directed at entire groups and tell every member of the group, 'Stay away or you'll be next.' I'm not at all sure Brian Murphy fits into this stereotype of thrill seeker, but there's lots out there who do. It's a major issue for our office to deal with."

"What does Lenny Zakim at the Anti-Defamation League say?" my mom asked when my father took a breath and stopped talking. "I mean, that organization is supposed to be a watchdog for anti-Semitic activities. Lenny should be on top of this whole graffiti scene."

"He is. He's worried but doesn't want to panic. He did say that a new ADL report showed that hate crimes in Massachusetts, by and large, are being committed by kids in the neighborhoods. Not by organized hate groups. This report goes with Lenny's theory that the only way we're going to prevent bias crimes is by educating youngsters about the destructiveness of racism. He's hoping we'll come up with an indictment against this kid that shows he didn't just commit an act of vandalism but rather a serious crime that has outraged the entire community."

"How long till you can get an indictment?" my mom asked.

"Probably a month," my dad answered. "There will be a preliminary hearing in the Rockville District Court, but our office is going to insist that the case goes directly to the grand jury where evidence will be heard for at least a week. I'm hoping that when the indictment is returned, the case will go before the superior court which is reserved for major felonies. That's an important change, thanks to the ADL's increased visibility in the community and the strong working relationship between them and the police. We want to make sure that the community sees our office and the police department as people they can rely upon. It's so important to have that trust."

I recognized the tone in my father's voice. My mom called it his soapbox tone, the kind he uses when he's running for re-election or being interviewed on television. Sometimes my dad forgets that he's talking to his family and not the voters or a reporter. But my mom always reminds him who he's talking to. "Enough of the speech for the media, Jack," she said. "Just give it to me straight. Is this little punk going to be put behind bars and the whole incident sewed up nice and tight or is there more here than meets the eye?"

"Oh, I wouldn't panic yet, Sue," my dad said, talking in his normal voice again. "We're just beginning to crack this case open. I'll know more tomorrow."

My mom's not the panicking type. I've seen Ricky's mother fall apart when we're an hour late coming home at night or if Ricky hurt himself or took some kind of risk. But my mother's calmer. Sure, she screams when I'm in the cage at a lacrosse game, but mostly she's pretty cool. Tonight, she wasn't looking very cool. I watched the two of them sitting there, letting their frozen yogurt melt in their bowls, talking quietly, and I felt a sharp stab of fear. I've heard that fear is icy cold, and that was how it seemed as it spread across my stomach. I knew it was late, but I needed to speak to Rachel.

"Try and get some sleep, Zack," my dad told me as I started to leave the kitchen. "This will all look a lot clearer in the daylight."

"Definitely," my mom agreed, but she didn't look like she believed him. I don't know why, but I leaned over and let my mom kiss my head for a second or two longer than usual. For a change, it felt good. I should have told my parents I knew Brian Murphy, but I didn't want to get into all that then.

Rachel picked up the phone in her bedroom on the second ring. Her voice was real sleepy. "They think they caught the kid who did the graffiti," I told her.

"Wow," she said, awake now. "That's good."

"I guess so," I said. "But the strange thing is it's this kid I know from lacrosse. He doesn't fit the pattern of someone who commits hate crimes. I mean, he's a kid, rather than a member of a hate group, and that does fit the pattern, but he's a kid who's never been in trouble before. That got my parents pretty bummed out."

"I can see why," she said. "And you sound bummed out, too, Zack."

"I am. It's kind of scary. You know, some kid I play against in lacrosse and he seems cool and then he goes and writes these gross things on a temple. My dad says hate crimes are on the rise. Hate crimes against Jews. I don't know why they hate us."

"Me neither. How could they hate an entire group of people when they don't even know us all?"

"It beats me. But the hate's out there. Brian Murphy is proof. Ordinary lacrosse player Brian Murphy. It's, like, who can you trust?"

"I guess not very many people," she answered. "Nothing seems safe."

"I know," I said. "I've never felt that way before. Have you?"

"Sometimes." Rachel's voice was soft again. I thought she might be falling back to sleep.

"You want to go back to sleep, Rachel? I'm sorry I woke you to tell you all this."

"It's okay, Zack," she whispered. "I'm just tired. See you tomorrow." And before I could say another word, she was gone, and I held a silent telephone in my hands. It was nearly two o'clock in the morning. I had a major test on *Death of a Salesman* in six hours, and I couldn't remember one thing about Willy Loman except that he cheated on his wife. Big deal. He has an affair and his eighteen-year-old son sees it and the kid decides not to go to college and ruins his life. Over a lousy affair. What was Miller talking about?

Then I remembered Miller's other work that I'd read a month ago, *The Crucible*. I'd been moved by that play. John Proctor had gone to the gallows, refusing to become part of the hysteria of seventeenth-century Salem. He wouldn't allow his confession to help the witch trials or destroy innocent friends. What a brave man, unafraid to die for what he believed. It had really gotten to me the way the Satan hysteria had overwhelmed Salem. Maybe there was some sort of hysteria in Rockville and it had made Brian write the graffiti. Maybe Satan was at work there.

I put down the telephone, turned off my light, and tried to go to sleep. But I was too worked up. All I could see when I closed my eyes was Rachel's braid, only every time I reached over to touch it, it was barbed wire. I couldn't believe that something so pretty could hurt so much, but it did. I had no choice but to stop touching it, but the blood kept covering my hands. Me and Lady Macbeth. When my alarm went off at 6:30, I was glad to escape from the painful world of my dreams. "Macbeth hath murdered sleep," I heard in my mind, and I could also hear Mr. Levy reciting that awesome soliloquy in his terrific voice. But the words only chilled me, and I had a horrible feeling that this day was going to be as icy as the night that had preceded it.

9

Rachel wasn't in school on Monday. I called her house during my first free period. Mrs. Levy answered and told me Rachel had a migraine and couldn't come to the phone. I wondered if I'd given her a migraine when I'd woken her out of a sound sleep and told her about Brian Murphy. Ricky said he doubted it. "She was probably getting it before you called her," he said during lunch. "My mom gets migraines and she's like nuts for days before they actually come. That's probably why Rachel was acting so weird on the phone. Why don't you send her some white roses? That'll score you some serious points."

One great thing about Ricky is his way of calming me down when I get worked up. He's a very rational guy. Rick says he wants to be a shrink, and I always tell him he'll make a great one. I accepted his opinion about the migraines, as well as about the roses. It cost me over twenty bucks, but I had the flowers delivered in a vase to her house. They included a note which read, *I'm thinking about you. But don't think about me because I want that headache of yours to go away so I can see you soon. Love, Zack.* Actually, I wanted to deliver the roses myself after school, but I had a game at three o'clock against Rockville. My mom came to the game with some huge dog that looked like a mix between a golden retriever and a German shepherd, along with a video camera strapped around her shoulder. There's all kinds of posted signs around the lacrosse fields forbidding dogs in the area, but they never seem to bother my mom. Plus, no one ever says anything to her about the dogs she brings. Of course, that's probably because the mutts are often the same size as most people. I wish she wouldn't attract so much attention to herself with those dogs, but, hey, that's my mom and there's no way anyone's going to change her. Plus, all my friends think it's the balls the way she saves animals from being put to sleep, and some of them even bet with each other about which animal she'll bring to the next game.

Anyway, the game was a cakewalk for us. We swamped the Rocks, 8-1, and I barely worked up a sweat. I was so concerned about Rachel that it didn't occur to me until halfway through the third quarter that we were playing Brian Murphy's team. That's because without him, they were barely average. I was walking off the field after the final quarter when Tony Caruso, the Rockville goalie, jogged over to me. "We stunk up the field today, huh?" he hollered to me as I gathered up my stuff.

"Naw, you guys were good," I said jokingly. "It's just that I was unstoppable."

"Aw, you were okay," Tony said, walking beside me off the field. "But your defense wasn't too bad either. I wouldn't have minded having them on my side today. Anyway, we were kind of demoralized. You heard what happened to our top-scoring attackman, didn't you?"

I stopped walking and looked at him for a second. The kid's name was Caruso. Even I knew that wasn't a Jewish name. I felt my back stiffen. For a minute, I was unsure what to say. Was he going to make an anti-Semitic remark to me? No one ever had before. Was he going to say Brian was getting a bum rap or that he deserved what he got? I was tongue-tied. Tony made it easy for me. "Can't believe he'd do a stupid thing like that," he continued. "Not Brian."

" 'Stupid' is putting it pretty mildly," I replied. "I think 'disgusting' is more like it."

"Yeah," Tony agreed. "But, man, someone is going to pay for that stunt. He's a good buddy of mine."

We'd reached the end of the field. Tony's bus was waiting, filled with his sullen-looking teammates. My teammates were chilling on their backs on the grass behind the bus. I looked at Tony and reached out to shake his hand, but he suddenly drew back and looked directly at me. "Your dad's the district attorney, isn't he?" he asked. I nodded. I knew he knew the answer. "I thought so," he played on. "So, I guess that means you're all involved with this case."

"I don't get involved in my dad's cases," I said. "But I am Jewish." I never said things like that, but there was something about the direction of this conversation that was beginning to make me feel defensive.

"Yeah, I know that," Tony said. "It's just that, like I said, Brian's a good buddy. And this is a rank deal he's going through. I figured it might help for me to give him any information that might cheer him up. I mean, look, maybe he didn't really do it like they said he did. Hey, I'm messing this whole thing up. I just wanted to tell you that Brian wants to talk to you. He remembers you from that lacrosse camp. You know, just two lax players rapping. How about meeting him at my house tonight? Around six."

I didn't know what to say. Suddenly, the bus driver started to honk the horn. Tony glanced over at the bus and then back at me. "Here," he said, handing me a piece of paper. "Here's my address. If you can come, man, it would be stellar. And you know what else I was thinking?"

I shook my head. I had no idea what else this guy could possibly be thinking.

"I was just thinking about your little brother," he continued. "Sam. I saw him at the game today. He sure cheers on his big brother. It's nice you two get along. I've got a big brother. He takes care of me. Like if anything ever happened to me, or was going to happen to me, he'd be right there for me. You gotta take care of your own family 'cause, if you don't, who will? Look, I gotta go." He swaggered over toward the bus. Just before he got on, he stopped and turned around. "Great game, Stone," he yelled to me before he disappeared inside the yellow bus.

As the bus pulled out of the parking lot, I had a sinking feeling in my stomach. Unless I was losing my mind, that guy had just threatened me. Me and Sam. I needed to repeat every word he had said to my father. But first, I had to talk to Rachel and find out what her deal was. Then, I would worry about Tony Caruso and Brian Murphy and, more importantly, Sam.

I sprinted the two miles to Rachel's house, my lacrosse equipment dangling off my back. Her mother told me she was asleep. She didn't mention the roses. "I'd love to see her for just a minute," I pleaded. "I won't stay long or anything like that, I promise."

"Oh, no, I'm not waking her up for anyone," Mrs. Levy stated. I noticed that even though it was after five, she wasn't cooking dinner. Mr. Levy's car was in the driveway, but I didn't see him sitting in his den and he wasn't going out of his way to say hello to me. The whole house just seemed . . . different. Cold. Unhappy. I hadn't realized how comfortable I was beginning to feel in this house until that moment. There were no smells, no music, no smiles, no discussions . . . and, worst of all, no Rachel. It was a bummer. I left quickly. Mrs. Levy hardly seemed to notice.

Instead of going home to phone my father, I walked over to Ricky's. I couldn't explain what had come over me, but the minute I left Rachel's house, all I thought about was Tony Caruso's house. It was as if my brain knew it could only handle just so much, and the situation with Rachel was taking up an awful lot of space. I had to drop that issue altogether in order to figure out what I was going to do. But by the time I arrived at Ricky's, I knew I had to go over to Tony's. It wasn't just his threat about Sam, although I certainly couldn't ignore that. I just felt as if I needed to try and fix some of the mess around me. I had a funny feeling something besides a migraine was bugging Rachel. And the whole graffiti thing was beginning to overwhelm me. I knew my dad would be furious at me for talking with Brian and for not telling him about Tony's threat, but I couldn't help it. Maybe if I met with Brian and found out what made him tick, I could explain it to Rachel, and she'd feel better. And if I went over to Tony's, I wouldn't have to worry about Sam.

Ricky was watching MTV with Patsy when I got to his house. "Can you drive me over to Rockville?" I asked him as he walked into his kitchen to get me a Coke. Ricky is seven months older than me and had had his license for over a month. His parents let him use one of their cars all the time. I sure envied him for his wheels.

"What for?" he asked.

"To see this guy about the graffiti thing."

If Ricky had asked me such a favor, I might have asked a few questions, but Rick just shrugged and replied, "Sure," which was a good thing since I never could have explained what I was doing anyway.

A half hour later, the two of us were heading down Loring Avenue in downtown Rockville, looking for number 15. We found the Caruso house easily. It was a gray, two-family house in serious need of a paint job. The Carusos lived on the first floor. "You want me to wait in the car?" Ricky asked as I started to get out of the car.

"No way," I said. "I could use you inside, buddy."

Ricky shrugged and followed me into the entrance hall of the house. Tony Caruso opened the door of his house before I had a chance to knock. I hadn't realized how huge he was. Everybody looks big in lacrosse stuff, with shoulder pads and helmets. My goalie equipment must add fifteen pounds to my frame. But Tony Caruso was as big without his goalie equipment as he was with it on. I stole a quick look back at Ricky. He looked awfully small. Funny, I'd never noticed that before.

"Hey, good to see you, man," Tony greeted me. Then he noticed Ricky who was standing in back of me. "Who's your buddy?" he asked.

"This is Rick Berg," I said, and Rick extended his hand.

Tony kind of bit his lip and nodded. He sure looked big—as if he were growing by the second. I wondered why I hadn't asked Cutter Lavoie to come with me. Cutter weighed a good 250. And he drove a pickup truck.

"Well, you guys come in and see Brian," Tony said, and Ricky and I followed him into the living room. Ricky stayed behind me which made me nervous. Actually, the whole house made me nervous. It was a mess. The kitchen we walked through had dirty dishes in its sink and a weird smell. Beer cans and newspapers covered the top of the coffee table in the den. And the furniture in the living room looked lived in, all right.

There were nasty tears in the couch and one of the drapes was hanging at a weird angle. I wondered if it was an apartment where Tony lived with a friend or something—or maybe with his big brother who never had any problem protecting his little brother. It seemed hard to believe there could be a Mrs. Caruso who would live with such a mess.

Brian Murphy was sitting on a kitchen chair in a corner of the living room. I'd never seen him without his lacrosse helmet—even at lacrosse camp. I hadn't realized what a good-looking guy he was. He sort of looked like Tom Cruise, only taller. But he didn't look like a choirboy to me. There was a funny look on his face. Kind of a sneer. Right away, I had this funny feeling that maybe there were two Brian Murphys: one, who was the son of the dentist and nursery school teacher, and the other who was Tony Caruso's good buddy.

Tony Caruso's good buddy stood up and came over to Ricky and me. Or, should I say, to me and to the kid who seemed determined to stay two steps behind me during this entire visit. "Hey, thanks for coming, man," Brian said. "Appreciate it."

I noticed that both Brian and Tony were wearing baseball caps with yellow and green emblems on them. Kind of strange-looking emblems, sort of a combination of a grasshopper and a bumblebee. I wasn't sure what the emblem was, but it didn't look friendly. I didn't know why I felt that way—maybe it was the condition of the Caruso house or the way Ricky was slinking around behind my back—but the hats seemed to match my feeling of discomfort. "No problem," I answered him. "What can I do for you?" All I wanted was for him to tell me real quickly what he wanted, so Ricky and I could get into his mom's Honda and hightail it back to Bromley. I had suspected I was nuts to go to this kid's house. Now I knew it for a fact.

"Well, that's kind of complicated." Brian sort of whistled through his teeth for a minute. "Why don't you two sit down?"

I was glad he noticed Ricky. "Sure," I said, "and, by the way, this is Rick Berg. He's a tennis player for Bromley High." Now, I've said a lot of dumb things in my life but that had to be one of my all-time stupidest. I glanced at Rick. He agreed with me. "He knows my dad real well, too." Another remark of the same quality. I needed to be chloroformed before I spoke another word. I sat down on the torn couch. The BHS tennis player and good pal of my dad's sat down beside me.

Strangely enough, Brian didn't even blink over my dumbness. Instead, he just nodded, as if what I'd said made perfect sense. "Yeah, well, I appreciate the two of you coming. This has been a real scene for me. You know, the police came into my house yesterday around nine o'clock in the morning. Man, I was sound asleep. My parents were getting ready to go play some tennis and suddenly this cruiser pulls up and these two cops come to the front door and ask for me. My parents almost croaked. You have to know my parents. This is not their scene at all. Anyhow, these two cops come in and tell my parents to get me. My dad flies into my room like he's on fire and tells me the cops want to see me. So I throw on my sweats and book downstairs, and before I know what's happening, these two dudes are talking about a search warrant, and they head into my room, and they're there for like an hour, while my parents keep pacing around, looking like they're going to have heart attacks. 'What's this about, Brian?' my old man keeps asking me, like I've got some idea.

"Anyhow, the cops finally leave and tell me to stay put and sure enough an hour later, they're back, only this time they've got this warrant for my arrest. They start reading me my rights, just like in the movies, and before I have any idea what's happening, I'm sitting in the back of the cruiser heading to the police station with them. This time I'm positive my parents are going to have strokes on the spot, but instead they get hold of my uncle John who's a hotshot lawyer and he meets us down at the station. There's a lot of talking going on, and for a while there I thought I was heading to the clinker; but then my uncle tells me we're out of there. I'm like dazed over the whole thing, but when we finally get home, my uncle explains to me that I've been accused of writing some junk on a Jewish place and I may go to jail for the rest of my life. Yesterday, my uncle mentions the district attorney and says his name is Stone and he's from Bromley. I put two and two together and remember you from lacrosse camp and thought maybe you could help me figure out this mess."

Mess? He thought this was a mess? That was putting it mildly. I was totally confused by his long-winded soliloquy, which I figured even Hamlet would have a hard time matching, even when he was in the midst of his madness. There wasn't the slightest way I could figure out this guy anyhow. I guess he sort of did look like a choirboy. A big seedy choirboy, that is. He was an excellent lax player and, like my father had said, a top student. His story about the police was harsh. His words, I could relate to, but his eyes were cold. I couldn't get a handle on this kid. Maybe if we'd met under different circumstances, maybe spent more time together at lacrosse camp, I could have gotten to know him. But, here, in this place, he made me wicked nervous. Like if I didn't say the right thing, me and Sam and Ricky were canned dog food. Still, I couldn't help feeling bad for him. When I didn't look at his eyes, he didn't seem like a kid who would write the names of seven concentration camps on the door of a temple. His clothes, his sneakers, his haircut, they were all cool. He looked pretty much like most of the kids I hung around with, which was more than I could say for his friend Tony Caruso, who looked like a sleaze bag. I'd come there hoping to get some answers, but all I found were more questions.

Before I could spit out one word, my pal Ricky sprang to life. Standing and moving more to my side than before, but still in my shadow, he had no trouble responding to Brian's story. "That sure sounds sick, man," he said. "But I know the Stones real well. One thing Mr. Stone does not do is talk about his cases in front of his family. I remember one case that had to do with some guy my mother knows, and Mr. Stone wouldn't even help her get some information. That's the kind of dude he is. Right, Zack?"

"Yeah," I agreed. "He doesn't talk about this stuff at all. I got to tell you, whatever I know about your case is what I read in the paper. I wish I could help you more."

"Well, you could." Tony was talking to me now. "Remember, the three of us play the same sport, man, and we should help each other all we can. You and Brian were camp buddies. We're not asking you to make your father break the law. We just want to know if you think Brian is in deep. 'Cause he's real confused. He didn't do it and he's gonna be fried 'cause someone thinks he did. Now, come on. You must know something about the way your father's office works."

"I wish I did," I said. "But I don't. I know a bit about search warrants and usually you can't get one unless you have reason to search the suspect's house. Do you know what they found in your room?"

Brian and Tony looked at each other before Brian answered. "They found a couple of paintbrushes and some lists of names of concentration camps," he said. "But I got to tell you, man. I never saw them before in my life. When my uncle told me about them, I almost dropped."

"Someone's out to get Brian," Tony said.

"Do you have any idea who it is?" Ricky asked. He seemed more relaxed now. At least, he wasn't rolling back and forth on the heels of his shoes.

Brian looked at Ricky as if he were seeing him for the first time. "Actually, I can think of one or two guys," he answered.

"Tell him the whole deal," Tony said.

Brian nodded. "Yeah, I better level with you guys. You see, I hung out with this girl who was Jewish, and she went to that temple. We were together for a while, but when we broke up, things were pretty bad. Her name's Beth Levine, and her folks are big at that temple place. They never liked me. When Beth and I split, we said some evil things to each other. I don't want to go into the whole thing, but, trust me, Beth and I aren't tight now. If anyone would want to bust me, it would be Beth and her parents."

Tony jumped in the minute Brian paused. "I heard that Beth is kind of psyched over this mess," he said. "One of her friends hinted that Beth might be involved. Like she wouldn't be surprised if Beth either did the whole thing or had somebody do it for her so she could frame Brian."

It sounded like something out of a movie. "Well, your uncle sure should get hold of Beth's buddy," Ricky said. "She's an important witness."

"Absolutely," I agreed. "I know that even if she refuses to testify, you can get her subpoenaed."

"Yeah, we could maybe do that," Brian said. "But I need you to tell me if your old man's gonna go after this case in a big way. My uncle said it all depends on how your dad's office looks at it. They may decide to make it a huge case or they might throw it in the back of the closet. I figured you could answer that question for me."

I knew the answer to his question was going to tick Brian off. I also knew it was a bad idea for me to be the one to make him angry. I shrugged. "I wish I knew that, guys," I said. "I don't. But, look, I'll see what I can find out and if it's anything that might help, I'll let you know."

"That's not good enough." Tony wasn't smiling any longer. And Ricky wasn't visible any longer. "We're gonna need more than just a few 'ifs' from you guys. We gotta know that for this game, we're on the same team."

If I'd been feeling a little shaky before, I was totally freaked out now. We were into the big time now. And I'd never felt smaller. Now I had only one thing on my mind, the same thing that was in the back of my mind from the minute I'd walked into 15 Loring Avenue: escape. Why on earth had I come to this place? What was the matter with me? "Like I said, I'll help you all I can," I repeated, noticing how far away the door to the apartment seemed to have moved. "I'll check with my dad and call you dudes when I get a beat."

Brian looked at Tony. Tony looked at Brian. Brian looked at me. Tony looked at me. I'm sure both Tony and Brian would have looked at Ricky, but he was in his invisible mode at that moment. Tony appeared ready to say something, but Brian put his hand on Tony's arm and Tony's mouth locked up. "How 'bout you call me around ten tonight?" Brian said, showing a slight smile. He sure had straight teeth. But, then, his father was a dentist. "Here's my number." He handed me a piece of paper with his phone number on it. "I'll be waiting."

"Sure thing," I said, extending my hand first to

Brian, then to Tony. Their handshakes were so firm, my hand felt like a piece of wood trapped in a vise, but I didn't flinch. I had faced lacrosse balls aimed at my neck. I was not a flincher. Then again, I thought, as I turned around and headed for the door, I wore pads and a helmet whenever I played lax. Away from the field, I had no protection. "We'll be in touch."

"*We* will not be in touch," Ricky said as soon as we reached the safety of his mom's car. He came back to life the second he locked the doors of the car. "*We* will not do anything. You're in this one all alone, pal. There are a lot of things I'm willing to do for you, but returning to that house is not one of them. For the life of me, I can't think of one reason you took your life—and mine, don't forget—into your hands and walked into that joint."

Ricky pulled out of the parking space so quickly I barely had time to grab hold of my seat belt. "I don't know why either. Tony asked me after the game. I just didn't think about it." I did know, however, that I shouldn't tell Ricky that Tony had threatened Sam. Not if I wanted to get out of his mom's car alive.

"Amazing!" Ricky said. "You must have been hit on the head a few too many times during the game today."

"Maybe," I agreed. "That was one uncool scene. But it's history."

"Uncool!?" Ricky was practically shouting now. It seemed strange. His being hyper and my remaining, at least on the surface, calm. It was as if we had switched personalities. "You call that *uncool?* I call that a scene from hell! It almost got ugly. I don't know if you were aware of what was happening there, but in case you weren't, let me give you a clue. I'll grant you, those two guys didn't fit the bill of your typical graffiti writers. No way. They're definitely innocent of scribbling evil messages on a temple. That's not their style. Why? 'Cause they're ax murderers! And, believe me, there were axes stashed in that rat-infested apartment. We're lucky to have escaped from that hole with our heads still attached to our necks. Now, tell me, what do you have planned for your next routine? A visit to Attica? 'Cause, I'm sorry to tell you this, but you'll have to ask your mom to drive you there. These wheels are no longer at your service. Find someone else for your suicide missions, Zack."

"Look, Ricky, I'm sorry about what happened." Ricky was beginning to freak me out. I'd never seen him drive so terribly. He practically hit a bus that was pulling away from a curb ahead. "I had no idea that was going to happen. I just went to see if I could find out what made Brian tick. I thought I could get Rachel out of her funk with a nice news report about him. But I didn't get jack. Now I promise you, I'll speak to my father and that'll be the end of it."

"Oh, great." Ricky appeared ready to take out another school bus that had the right of way at the intersection. The bus honked, and Ricky sped up, narrowly avoiding a five-car collision. "So you'll tell your dad what those guys said. Then you'll call Brian at ten and tell him your father said they should back off. Are you nuts? First of all, you can't tell your father what happened. How do you think he's going to handle the fact that you went to this kid's house? You don't have to be a genius to know that was one sad move on your part. Look, you've got to tell those guys your father's not involved in the case and you don't know the guy who's handling it."

"Brian's uncle already knows my dad's handling it. I have to talk to my dad, Rick."

Ricky slowed down a bit. We were just a few blocks

from my house. "I don't like those guys, Zack," he said. "They're trouble."

"I agree," I said. "But I can't handle them alone. Look, I'm sorry I brought you into this in the first place, but I promise, you're out of it as of now. I'll handle the rest with my dad. Just chill. Okay, Rick?"

Ricky pulled up to my driveway. "I just don't like those guys," he repeated. His voice was normal now, but he looked awfully small behind the wheel of his mom's Honda.

"I don't like them either," I said. "Thanks for going out there with me. I'll buzz you later."

"Call me as soon as you get off the phone with Brian," he said.

"You got it," I shouted as I jumped out of his car. "Five past ten."

10

At ten that night, I wasn't talking to Ricky Berg or Brian Murphy or my dad. I was talking to Rachel Levy and trying to understand what had happened to make our relationship fall apart.

"I'm not angry with you," Rachel was saying in an irritatingly calm voice. "I just need some space."

One thing about Pam. When she was angry with me, I heard it. And so did anyone within a ten-mile radius. Rachel was quiet and unemotional. It was driving me crazy. "Space?" I repeated. "I didn't know I was crowding you."

"You weren't," she insisted. "It's just me. I'm feeling squished. Please, Zack, don't feel bad. I still want us to be friends."

I couldn't believe my ears. I was getting dumped. This warm, funny girlfriend of mine was giving me the heave-ho. And for no reason at all. I'd been so relieved when she answered the phone in her normal voice and said she was glad I had called. Now, I was wishing I had stayed at 15 Loring Avenue. What had happened there was less horrible than what was happening to me now. The funny thing was Rachel had sounded all right—until I started to tell her about my encounter with

Brian and Tony. Then her voice had turned sickeningly calm, and before I knew what was happening, she needed space and me, the miserable crowder, was being shoved away.

"I'll be glad to be your friend," I told her. "But, as a friend, I need to know what I did to make you want to end our other relationship."

"You didn't do anything, Zack."

She was sounding more impatient now. Like she'd love to be off the phone and watching TV. Or talking to another friend. My stomach was sinking.

"It's me. I'm weird. You're a great kid. I really like you. I just don't want to go out with anyone right now. Can't we be friends?"

"Fine," I said, hating the sound of my voice. "I'll be whatever you want." It was whiny, pathetic, but then again, that was me, the pathetic dumpee. "I'll call you once a month on a Tuesday at seven-thirty in the evening, if that's what you want. Or Sunday afternoons between one-thirty and one-forty-five. Or I'll send you a letter on the first Tuesday of every month and come visit you for twenty-five minutes on the third Wednesday. I'll be a great friend. But I need to know what's going on here. You're upset with me because of the graffiti, aren't you?"

"Why would I feel that way, Zack?" Rachel asked, rather edgy.

I couldn't help it, but I was glad to have gotten a rise out of her. "Because you and I were fine until I woke you up last night and told you that the police had arrested Brian Murphy. Then you started to act weird and you didn't come to school today and you wouldn't talk to me when I came to your house. And now you were okay for a few minutes, but when I told you about Tony's house, you dumped me. So, what else could I be thinking except that maybe that conversation did a number on you?"

"I can't explain it, Zack. I wish I could. I want to be your friend, but if you don't want us to be friends, I understand. I have to go now."

Before I could say another word, I heard the click. My stomach felt as if I had just entered the final stretch of a roller-coaster ride. I wanted to throw up. I wanted to throw something against the wall. I called Ricky. He answered on the first ring.

"Man, I've been waiting to hear from you," he said. "It's almost quarter to eleven. Were you on the phone with Brian all this time?"

"Brian?" I asked, momentarily confused. "Brian who?"

"Are you crazy! Brian Murphy, you idiot. The ax murderer who's got your name on his newest ax. Stop kidding around with me, dude, and tell me what he said when you called him at ten."

"I didn't call him. I called Rachel. And she dumped me."

There was silence on the phone. Then Ricky whistled. Kind of a low, deep whistle. "Hey, man, I'm sorry," he said when he was through whistling. "That sucks. That chick was mad for you. What happened?"

"I don't know," I said. "Ever since I called her last night to tell her Brian Murphy had been arrested, she's been acting like a weirdo. Now she says she wants us to be friends. If *I* can handle it. She needs space. It's over."

"Maybe you should call Diane Halpert," Ricky said. "They're best friends. She's cool. She'll give you the scoop."

"I might," I said. "I just don't think I can do that now. Maybe tomorrow."

"Speaking of tomorrow, I hate to add to your case,

but you might not be alive tomorrow if you don't call Brian right now. I know you're all upset about Rachel, but this is your life we're talking about, not your social life. Your real, live, breathing life. Did you really forget all about that phone call?''

''Yeah, I did,'' I said. But the chill was starting to return to my bones. Rachel's voice had drained the blood out of my body, but Ricky's was making it return. Only it was an icy blood flowing through my veins. How could I have forgotten Brian Murphy? It was time to pull a Rachel, develop a massive migraine, and crawl under the covers for a year or two. But I wouldn't be safe even there, not from the blows to my head from Brian Murphy nor the stabs to my heart from Rachel Levy. I was dead meat. I might as well let Brian finish off what Rachel had started. ''But I'll call him. Now.''

Brian answered on the first ring. It was like he and Ricky had been sitting on their phones. ''I've been waiting to hear from you for an hour,'' he told me. ''You have trouble telling time?''

''No,'' I answered, trying not to sound like the pathetic wimp who had just been dumped by his girlfriend. It was funny but Rachel's call might have given me some new strength. I wasn't going to let this creep steamroller me, too. ''I've been busy.''

''Too busy to talk to your old man about a fellow lax player's troubles?'' There was no doubt, Brian was slipping into gear to roll right over me. His tone was menacing.

''My father's not home yet,'' I told Brian. That wasn't the truth. My father was home. He'd come home while I was talking to Rachel. He'd knocked on my door, but I'd been too wrapped up in being dumped to talk to him then.

''When will he be home?''

"I don't know. He works real late some nights. Some nights he doesn't get home 'till after midnight."

"Well, that's no problem. I'm a late-nighter. I don't care what time your father gets home. Talk to him about my case and call me back. Got it?"

"Listen, Brian, I know you're upset about your case. And I'd like to help you. But I don't see how I can. My father's an honest guy. He's not going to give me any information that he doesn't give the press first. If I rub him the wrong way about your case, he'll go the other way and get more hard-nosed. The best thing I can do for you is keep my ears open and my mouth shut. If I learn anything, I'll call you. Capeesh?"

"No way. I need help and you're the one who's gonna give it to me. I don't care what time your father gets home. You ask him how things are looking about my case and you get back to me with his exact words. And don't give me any crap about his getting hard-nosed. I'm hard-nosed. And so is Tony. And if you know what's good for you and your little brother, you'll do what you're told. Okay?"

The knock at my door was so loud, Brian had to have heard it. I tried to ignore it, but my father's voice was louder than the knock. "Are you still up, Zack?" he was practically screaming.

"Hey, you're in luck," Brian said, before I could shut my father up. "Say hi to your dad for me and call me back. I'll be waiting, pal."

I opened the door to my father as soon as I hung up the phone. He was dressed for bed in the running shorts and tee shirt he always wears to sleep. He claims it saves time in the morning when he gets up to run if he sleeps in his running clothes. For a while now, my brother Sam has been sleeping in running shorts and a tee shirt, too. He never goes running with my father but he does sleep in the same clothes. Someday, I'll figure Sam out, but that day is a long way away. Of course, if I didn't do something about Brian Murphy, Sam's sleepwear would be about the least important thing in that poor kid's life. Anyhow, my dad walked into my room wearing dark blue Converse shorts and a Cornell tee shirt. Both he and my mom graduated from Cornell and have every tee shirt Cornell has printed.

"I heard you had a great game against Rockville," he said as he sat down on my bed. "I felt terrible I couldn't get there, but Mom said you were unbelievable."

That game seemed like it had taken place ten years ago. Could that really have been this afternoon? Before 15 Loring Avenue and Rachel's dump? "Yeah, it was a good game," I said. "The whole team played great."

"Yeah, she said Dana and Keldog were fantastic on defense. And Paul scored four goals in a row. You guys are really on your way to quite a season. You got a late start, but I think you're going all the way to the states. When's your next game?"

"Thursday. In Manchester."

"Too bad," he said, shaking his head. "I'll be in court all day in Rockville. I doubt I can break away for that one either. I'll ask Sam to video it for me if he doesn't have a baseball game. I hate missing your games."

"Don't worry. We're at home next week. And I'll get the coach's video for you. Sam can stay home and do his homework. Hey, I'm curious. Will you be in court with that graffiti case on Thursday?"

"Yeah. We'll be doing an arraignment."

"On that Brian Murphy?"

"Yeah. I was just thinking. He plays for Rockville. Did he play today?"

"No."

"That's too bad. He could have. He's out on bail. I

guess his parents decided he shouldn't play a sport while this whole thing is going on. Unless his coach made a decision not to let him play. Hey, did you play against Brian last year?''

''No. Not that I can remember.'' Again, the lie. For no reason. Just some crazy need to hide that information from my father. ''But about his parents. You said they seemed pretty nice, didn't you?''

''Yeah. They seemed like decent people. And Brian seemed like a nice kid. Like I've been saying all along, none of this makes sense.''

''What do you mean a 'nice kid'?'' I asked.

''Oh, I don't know. Just something about him that rubbed me the right way. But it's funny you ask. Patty disagrees. She says he's sneaky. A real chameleon. You know what she means?''

''That he changes his personality to suit whoever he's with?''

''Yeah. She said she heard him talking to his mother and he was fresh. But when his father came into the room, he was Mr. Choirboy. She's probably right. It's funny. The last thing I want is to develop an attachment for that kid. It must be because of you.''

''Because of me?'' I heard my voice rise. ''What do you mean?''

''Oh, I guess because he's your age. I can't help thinking it could be my kid out there, being bombarded by the law. That's ridiculous, I know. That could never be you. Although, like your mother always says, 'Never say never.' ''

My dad was stretched out at the end of my bed now. He does that a lot. He comes in to talk to me and the next thing I know he's asleep on the end of my bed. My mom always comes in and collects him, which is a good thing for me since my bed isn't that big and my dad snores. But I usually feel good when he sleeps on my bed. I can't explain it; it just makes me feel safe.

My dad wasn't asleep yet. I could have gotten him completely awake by telling him what happened today between me and Brian. It would be the right thing to do. Or I could have let him in on what was going on with me and Rachel. He'd try and help me sort all that out, too. But I didn't have the strength to bring up either topic. My dad was exhausted. And I wasn't operating at full steam either.

"It does seem strange," I said as the other body on my bed became more relaxed. "I mean, how could some normal kid from a normal family do such a hateful thing? You must be right. There must be more than meets the eye."

"We're searching for that," he said sleepily. "Peer pressure. Thoughtlessness. A little bit of both, with a few other ingredients thrown in. My whole office is trying to figure it out."

And that was it. He was out cold. I could have woken him up with some facts from my own life, but I didn't. Instead, I took my telephone receiver off the hook and placed it inside a drawer of my dresser, stuck between my underwear so I wouldn't have to hear that loud buzzing sound. I took out my math book and reviewed for the next day's quiz.

When my mother came in to get my father, it was after midnight and I knew my quadratic equation backward and forward.

My mother looked half asleep, but she studied me intently as she stirred my dad. "You look funny," she said to me before my father woke up. "You were acting strange at dinner, too. What's up?"

I couldn't believe that woman. It's like she has this extrasensory perception into my personal life. Or else she's a witch, something I've suspected for a while now. "I'm fine," I lied, wishing I could open up my heart and tell her how miserable Rachel had made me and how scared Brian was making me. She, more than my father, could have helped me figure out what was going on with Rachel. But I didn't want her help. "I'm wiped out. If I don't get serious sleep, I'm going to flunk a huge math test tomorrow."

That did it. No matter how worried my mother might be about my personal life, when it came to sleep before a test, she voted for sleep. She nodded, yanked my poor father's arm, and led him, half unconscious, out of my room. I left the phone in the drawer and turned off my light, certain of two things: I wouldn't get five seconds decent sleep and Brian Murphy would find a way to get his body and his ax into my bedroom.

•11

I aced my math test. I couldn't believe it, I got an *A+*. The last thing I was thinking about when I walked into school was the quadratic equation. Yet, my mind was in rare shape and answered questions I didn't understand at all. But the rest of the day, I flunked royally.

Rachel was a pure *F*. Everywhere I turned there she was, looking pretty but as distant as Princess Di. First, we met outside my locker. She was walking by with Diane Halpert. Diane's look was a thousand times warmer than her royal friend's empty stare. It was one thing hearing Rachel explain we were now just friends. It was another thing seeing her smile blankly at me. Man, it hurt.

And it killed when we met after my math class, outside the gym, in the library, at lunch, and before French. She barely smiled each time, said, "Hi," and walked on by, hurrying to her next class as if she didn't know me. As if she hadn't sat on my lap in the backseat of Ricky's mother's car and wrapped her arms tightly around my neck less than a week ago. As if she hadn't called me at least two times each day, just to tell me she missed me. As if she hadn't left sweet notes in my locker, on my desk in math, French, history, and lit.

Twice, I tried to get her to talk to me, but each time, she resisted, offering me only a faraway smile. Ricky was as dumbfounded as I was. "She's the last chick I'd expect to diss you," he told me as he walked with me to lacrosse practice. He had a tennis match at three, but he knew I was bummed out and, unlike Rachel, hadn't declared me an undesirable. "Patsy said she'd ask Rachel what was up, if I want her to."

"No thanks," I said. "Rachel's not going to say anything. Actually, Rachel doesn't like Patsy that much. I mean, I'm sure she likes her more than she likes me, but that doesn't say much, does it?"

Ricky nodded, looking as confused as I felt. "No, I guess, it doesn't," he said. "But, listen, maybe I can say something. I'm in her French class. She sits near me. How 'bout tomorrow I ask her what the deal is?"

Rick's suggestion didn't cheer me up. But what could I say? Ricky was my best friend and he was offering to intercede for me with my girl. "Sure," I said. "Whatever you think."

"I'll do my best," he said. "But I got to tell you, this thing with Rachel is small potatoes compared to what's going on with Brian. You can't tell me that putting your phone off the hook is going to solve the problem with that dude and his animal trainer Caruso. You better tell your dad what's going on."

I just couldn't worry about Brian. In my most depressed moments, I imagined Brian coming into school and blowing my head off with a semi-automatic gun. As I lay dying on the corridor floor outside my locker, I could visualize Rachel racing over to my bloodied body as devastated as poor Juliet upon discovering Romeo's freshly poisoned body. "I will kiss thy lips," she would moan as she knelt beside me. "Haply some poison yet doth hang on them, To make me die with a restorative. Thy lips are warm." I almost told Ricky about it, but he had to rush off to his tennis match. It was probably a good thing or he might have dragged me off to Mr. Reynolds, our school psychologist, whose help I definitely needed.

The minute lacrosse practice ended and Mr. Wetherbee walked off the field, I saw Brian and Tony standing by a tree at the edge of the field. My first thought was to run like hell, but I didn't. Mostly because I was carrying the net and six lacrosse balls. Plus, I knew that no matter where I ran, they'd find me. My biggest regret was that they were going to murder me when Rachel wasn't around to scream out her love. Just my lousy luck.

Brian sauntered over to me, real slow, followed by Tony who looked like he had a gun in the pocket of his jeans jacket. "Hey, Stone," Brian called as he reached me. "Wait up, buddy."

I stopped walking and looked around for my teammates. I had heard the tone in Brian's voice. This wasn't the choirboy. Nor Mr. Average Teenage America. This was the evil kid Patty'd recognized. I couldn't believe it. All my loyal teammates were heading back to the locker room like nothing unusual was happening. Their goalie's life was in danger and they were going to grab their books and head home to eat dinner. Great. Let them see how well they would do without me in the net. Let the whole miserable world see how well it does without Zack Stone. "Sure," I answered my executioner, dropping the lacrosse balls at that moment. The truth was I was no longer carrying the net. It was carrying me. Or, rather, I was wrapped up in it, sort of like a bug caught in a spiderweb. I couldn't have run if I'd wanted to. "What's up?"

"What's up?" Tony repeated sarcastically, smiling at Brian as he spoke. "The kid wants to know what's up. Shall I tell him what's up?"

Brian had handed off the ball to Tony. He'd step

back and let Tony rip me to shreds. Mr. Choirboy with no blood on his hands, all the way. Brian smiled back and nodded vigorously.

"Yeah, I might as well tell him what's up since it sort of has to do with him, wouldn't you say?" Tony continued. Brian nodded again.

Man, I wished I wasn't all caught up in the net. I would have loved to have bashed in Tony's teeth. Funny, I'd never thought of myself as a violent person before. Oh, sure, I'd had my share of fights, but that had been during sixth and seventh grades, when I was proving myself to the kids in the middle school. And most of them hadn't been real fights. Just sort of pushing matches. "You want to fight?" one of us sixth-graders would say.

"Yeah, I want to fight," the other one would answer.

"Yeah, well, you picked the wrong guy for a fight," the first guy would answer.

"Oh, yeah," the second one would say. "How's that?"

And the banter would go on until one of us did a little pushing. And the pushing would continue until an adult or another kid broke it up. Or, if all else failed, a few blows would be exchanged. I had never minded that scene, because I had sensed early on that no one really liked to fight and everyone was looking for a way to avoid doing it without coming out like a wimp. Plus, I was okay in the fighting department. It was the same skill I used in the lacrosse net. Keep your eye on your opponent and figure out where he's throwing his fists or his ball before he does. Yet a good three years after my last fight, standing on the edge of the lacrosse field, my body wrapped up in a stupid net, I had no way of figuring out one thing about Tony Caruso's fists. I was outclassed here, but good.

"Look, Brian, if it had to do with last night—" I

said, but before I could get another word out, Tony was in my face.

"Yeah, it had to do with last night," Tony said with serious bite in his words. "It had a lot to do with last night. You see, my friend here tried your phone number about twenty times last night, right up until three o'clock in the morning. Then he fell asleep. He tried it around six when he woke up and guess what? It was still busy. Now, maybe you Stones got a lot of phone calls last night, or maybe you took the phone off the hook so my friend here couldn't get through. So what was going on with your phone last night?"

I saw no reason to lie. I was as good as dead, no matter what I said. "I took it off the hook," I admitted. "I couldn't help it. My father had to go back to his office last night before we could talk and I knew Brian would call and wake up my mother and I didn't want to get her involved in all this."

"All this?" Tony asked, moving even closer into my face. Man, I could smell the tuna fish sandwich he'd eaten earlier. "Now, do tell me exactly what you mean by 'all this' 'cause I'm a little confused right now." He looked back at Brian, who was loving this whole scene. "Hey, Murphy," he asked his good buddy, "you know what 'all this' might be?" Brian shook his head. "Guess that makes two of us," he told me. "So you better explain it real good to me and my friend."

"I meant your asking me to get information from my father about your case," I said, looking desperately toward the school. Not one of my miserable teammates was within view. "I tried to tell you my father doesn't give out information to anyone, not even to me. But you wouldn't listen. I wish I could help you, Brian, but I can't. My dad's not going to tell me anything at all. You're gonna have to wait till your indictment to find out what the district attorney's office is planning to do."

Brian jumped back like I'd slapped him. I glanced down quickly at my hands. They were hanging uselessly at my side as the net settled more firmly around my body. I was a caterpillar wrapped in a miserable cocoon, a spider trapped in his own web. "Indictment?" he repeated. "What do you know about my indictment?"

"Nothing," I said. I couldn't believe I'd let that slip out. It was yet one more example of how far over the edge Rachel had pushed me. "I don't know anything about your indictment. I just meant that there usually is an indictment after an arrest. Isn't that what your uncle told you?"

"My uncle said there'll be a preliminary hearing in the Rockville District Court," he said. "If your father's office insists it goes to the grand jury, evidence will be heard for around a week. Then, if an indictment is returned, the case'll go before the superior court which takes major felonies. He's hoping it won't come to that. It's all in your dad's hands."

I couldn't believe how much this kid knew. I'd heard my father talk about hearings and the district and superior courts and indictments for as far back as I could remember, yet I still didn't understand the happenings of the court. My luck, this kid did. A thug with brains. Of course, it was his life we were talking about. Obviously, he was smart enough to learn what he had to about his own future in the courtroom. "Look, I don't know too much about all that indictment stuff," I said, "but there's something here you don't understand. That's my dad's role in all this. He's the district attorney for our county, but that doesn't mean he makes all the decisions about every case that comes into his office. There's a whole staff of people there. I'm not sure he's that involved in your case. He's probably going to give some of the case work to the other lawyers in his office. It's not all his show."

"Yeah, well, that's where you're dead wrong," Brian said, backing off just a bit, away from me and my giant mosquito net. "Your father's personally involved in this case, all right. He's leading a big campaign against hate crimes. My uncle filled me in. Your old man wants to make sure anyone who shows prejudice against someone else is punished hard. And he's gonna use my case as the big example. The point is, Stone, I didn't write that graffiti. But even if I did, it's stupid to send me to jail for the rest of my life for something so lame. It was just a prank, a joke. Nothing to cause all the fuss your father's making. Now, are you starting to catch my drift?"

"Yeah, I catch your drift." I don't know why, but Brian's simple view of what had happened angered me more than his snarling words. I could see his goon standing behind me, but I didn't care. I had something to say to this creep. How had I ever thought he might be an okay guy? "And I don't agree with it. I didn't see the graffiti. But I don't think it was a prank. You insulted every person who belongs to that temple. You glorified a terrible time in history. I don't know what my father is planning, but if he's going to defend a law that you can't hurt some people because they're Jewish, I think that's great."

"You little Jew scumbag!" Before I could see what was happening, Caruso had me in a neck lock. His hands were pressing tightly around my neck, digging the lines of the net into my skin. At first, it felt as if my skin were being stripped off my neck. But that painful sensation faded quickly as my assailant's hands tightened against my throat, making it difficult for me to breathe. I tried to free my hands but they were too tangled in the net. It was all happening so quickly, I couldn't think. Suddenly, I was on the ground, my head hitting something very hard, but I could breathe a little despite the heavy load on my chest. I could see a blur in front of me. Brian was pulling Tony off me.

"Get off him, you animal!" Brian was yelling, and Tony was muttering obscenities, some of which I'd never heard before. "You're overdoing it. You're just supposed to scare him, not kill him!"

I struggled not to pass out, to concentrate on the little blur of blue sky above me. When I was able to breathe again, I realized Tony's body was off mine. I closed my eyes and a deep, dark sleep came over me, unlike any sleep I'd ever known before.

When I awoke, Dana Kessel was kneeling in front of me, mumbling something I couldn't understand.

"You okay, Zack?" I finally realized he was asking me. I wasn't all right. My throat ached, my head was screaming in pain, and I had rope burns on my neck and face. But I was alive. And that was a miracle to end all miracles. I nodded, but the nod made my head hurt even more. With Dana's help, I stood up, and together the two of us pulled the rest of the net off my body. "What happened to you, man?" Dana was asking me. "I saw two guys take off when I came back for my stick. Who were they? What happened?"

"It's a long story," I said when the latest wave of pain passed. "I'll tell you later." I let Dana lead me back into the empty locker room, grateful to be alive but certain I'd just received a reprieve from a horrible fate destined to rip what was left of my heart out of my body. I smiled at my melodramatic response, but, hey, I'd just been beaten up and practically strangled to death. But I was alive. I'd resisted the poison. I was entitled to a little melodrama. I'd never felt worse in my life, but for some strange reason, I'd never felt better. If only Juliet could see me now.

•12

I'd never seen my mother so upset. I mean, she gets mad plenty, but she totally lost it when Dana drove me home. She insisted on dragging me to Dr. Sontz's office. Dr. Sontz has been my pediatrician since I was born. The guy's as nice as they come, but he's also as old as they come. He's close to eighty, maybe even ninety, and his hands shake like crazy, but my mom swears there's no one like him. "He knows things younger doctors haven't even read about," she says when I complain about going to him. "I've trusted you and Sam to him since you were both born and you're both alive now, aren't you?"

I wonder if she'd think he was so terrific if she had to get an injection from those shaky hands. One of these days he's going to miss my arm and inject my left eyeball. Then, maybe, my mom will consider finding me and Sam a younger doctor. Even if it's one who doesn't know everything Dr. Sontz knows.

Dr. Sontz never shows much emotion, not even when Sam or I have a high fever or have been vomiting for three days. But when he saw my neck, he got all red. "What happened to you, Sam?" he asked me as soon as he got my mother out of the examining room, which wasn't that easy. It doesn't bother me that he calls me Sam; it's just his shaky hands that do me in. "Tell me the truth, boy."

"I got into a little fight at my lacrosse game," I told him. I'd told the same thing to my mother, but it hadn't calmed her down. "One of the guys got out of control, but I'm fine now."

"Those are serious marks around your throat, Sam," he insisted. "Someone was trying to finish you off, boy."

"Naw," I said. "He was just fooling around. Lacrosse is a rough game. Sometimes you all get carried away."

"And that bump on your head," he continued, looking into my eyes with his little flashlight till all I could see was red dots. "That was getting carried away, too?"

"Yeah," I said. I was beginning to feel a little nauseated.

"Well, I'm worried about you, Sam," he said, examining my neck with the flashlight. The dots went away, but now I was seeing a few stars. "I'm afraid you might have a concussion, son. I'm going to send you to the hospital for X rays. Hey, are you all right? What's—"

The next thing I knew I had thrown up all over Dr. Sontz's white jacket. He couldn't have been cooler. He just stepped back a few feet and got me a white basin and some paper towels and waited while I emptied my guts into the basin. When I was finished throwing up, my mother drove me to the hospital, averaging close to sixty m.p.h., where they X-rayed my head and decided to keep me overnight for observation. There was all kinds of talk about my filling out a police report, but when they realized whose son I was, the subject was dropped until my dad showed up.

By the time my father and Sam arrived, I was no

longer nauseated, but my body felt as if it had been through a war, a war it had lost. My father looked like he was going to cry when he saw me, but Sam was psyched about the intravenous bag hooked up to my right arm and explained all about it to me and my dad. I wasn't interested in hearing about my veins and the medications and the glucose and saline being pumped into them, but my dad perked up during Sam's medical lecture. Finally a nurse came in and agreed to let Sam inspect her tray of medications for the entire floor. I was relieved to see my brother take off.

"He's going to be a doctor, you know," my father said when we were alone.

"I thought he was going to be a rocket scientist," I said.

"Probably that, too," my father agreed. "But I'm not worried about your brother. I'm worried about you. I want to know exactly what happened to you, Zack."

And so I told him. The whole thing. From the visit to Loring Avenue to the scene at the lacrosse field. Including lacrosse camp with Brian and why I was worried about Sam, too. I'd never seen my dad look so upset.

"I can't believe it," he kept muttering during my explanation. Finally, when I was through, he said, "I'd resign my job if I thought this was ever going to happen again."

I was suddenly feeling very brave. "Oh, don't worry, Dad," I said. "I can handle it."

"Oh, no, you can't," he insisted. "You're out of your league, Zack. These two kids are in big time now. I can't believe how I underestimated Brian Murphy. But don't you worry about them. They're not going to harm you again. That much, I promise you."

"But it was just a fight," I said.

"No, it wasn't," he said. "It was intimidation and attempted murder."

"You mean, every time two kids get into a rumble, it's attempted murder? I think you're a bit off, Dad."

"Tony didn't punch you, Zack," my father said. "He tried to strangle you. The marks on your neck are proof of that. It's one thing to throw a punch. It's another to put your hands around someone's throat and squeeze as hard as you can. Especially when that person's caught in a net and can't protect himself. And Brian was more than an innocent bystander. He was an accomplice. And the threats against Sam can't be ignored. But don't worry about all those details. That's my job."

"But I do," I said. "Just promise me that this case won't be handled differently because I'm your son. I mean, if Tony had put his hands around someone else's neck besides the son of a district attorney, would it still be handled this way?"

"Absolutely," my father insisted. "I know what you're saying and I can appreciate where you're coming from. You have to live in this town. You don't want any special consideration because of me. I've told you a million times that it would never help that your father was the district attorney if you committed a crime. If anything, it would make matters worse because of the publicity." Then he sat down on my hospital bed and buried his face in his hands. I didn't know what to do, so I studied my intravenous bottle. Its contents sure were moving slowly.

"This whole case has me baffled," he said, speaking pretty normally once his face came out of his hands. "Every time I come close to understanding it, something new gets thrown into the pot. I was beginning to think this kid Brian Murphy was a front for someone else. He just doesn't fit the bill for a teenager who commits hate crimes. They're usually from blue-collar families and already have police records. Oh, sometimes they're just kids who get drunk and do something stupid, but usually they come from a family where they've been hearing ugly things about blacks and Jews and Hispanics since they were old enough to talk. But the Murphys don't fit that bill, either. They're decent people who don't appear prejudiced. It looks as if they've raised their only son in a decent manner, not that differently from the way your mother and I have raised you and Sam. But now, this. I was obviously dead wrong about this kid. He's a bad apple. Well, don't you worry, Zack. My office will make sure he pays for everything he did to you today."

My father looked like he was going to cry. "Hey, Dad," I said, anxious to get him away from any teary scene. "I might look bad, but I'm okay. It all happened so quickly I didn't even know what was going on. And you're right about Brian. Despite what happened, at times he does seem like a decent kid. I know that sounds crazy, but it was his friend Tony who tried to strangle me. He pulled Tony off me. Before all that happened, Brian and I were having sort of a good conversation. Well, until I disagreed with him. He's like two different people. And if things were different, I might have been able to have been friends with one of those people."

My father shook his head. "Do me a favor," he said as the nurse came in with another medication. Thank God, it was a pill, not another needle. "Promise me you'll be a doctor."

"A doctor?" I asked.

"Yes, a doctor," he repeated. "They get to work with sick people and make them well. It must be a wonderful feeling. I wouldn't know a thing about it, because even though district attorneys also get to work with sick people, they never make them well. They just make themselves sick. Oh, forgive me, Zack, I'm just having a minor breakdown.'' He stood up and smiled at the nurse who was trying to appear inconspicuous beside my bed, which wasn't easy since she weighed at least 250 pounds. ''I'll leave you two alone,'' he said. ''Don't worry, Zack. I'm fine. Just exhibiting a few signs of insanity and paranoia. They go with the job. You get some rest. I'll be back later tonight.'' He leaned over and hugged me and walked out of the room, looking, I was certain, a lot worse than me.

As it turned out, my father did not come back later that night. But I was so swamped with company, I never noticed. Ricky and Patsy and the entire lacrosse team including Coach Wetherbee showed up, with presents ranging from old copies of *Sports Illustrated* to chocolate frappes. Patsy brought a flower arrangement with humongous red and orange flowers that covered the entire shelf beside my bed. Her eyes got all filled up with tears when she saw me, and she kept telling me how much I looked like James Caan in *Misery,* lying in his bed just before the nutcase clobbered his leg. Man, that sure cheered me up. Two of my other friends, Todd Ellerin and T. J. Winick, also came. And so did Diane Halpert. Everyone it seemed, except the one person I would have given anything to see. Stupidly, I asked Diane how her best friend was, and she said, ''Oh, Rachel's fine. She has this huge test tomorrow.''

''I hope she does real well,'' I said sarcastically.

''Oh, she always does real well,'' Diane said, ignoring the anger in my voice. ''She studies wicked hard for every quiz and test. I don't know anyone who works as hard as her.''

''Me, neither,'' I agreed, and then we both shut our mouths about Rachel and talked about my scene at the field. It was like I was a hero. After everyone else left my room, Ricky told me they had arrested Tony and that he didn't have bail money and was in jail.

I was shocked. "How could they arrest him when I haven't even identified him?" I asked.

"Apparently Dana saw him and Brian leaving the field and reported it to the police. Can you believe it? Brian told the police what Tony had done and said he would testify about it in court if they wanted. Supposedly, he was a pussycat. I hope I don't get called into this whole thing. I never told my mother I took her car to Rockville yesterday. She'd have a conniption fit if she knew I parked her car on Loring Avenue. You know how crazy she gets."

I nodded and lay back on my bed. I was worn out from all my company. The extra-large nurse, who I decided actually did look like Kathy Bates in *Misery,* kept throwing each visitor out after a few minutes, but I was still exhausted. For some reason, though, she liked Ricky and allowed him to stay after everyone else, even, finally, my mom left. "I can't believe what's happened," I said. "I'm going to have trouble sleeping tonight."

"Yeah, I bet. But I've got to tell you you were pretty lame not telling your father what was going on from the beginning."

"I know," I agreed. "But I was distracted."

"That's another story," he said. "I happen to have a little information about that one."

I shot up into a sitting position. My head and neck stung like crazy, but I could handle it. "You spoke to Rachel? Why didn't you tell me right away?"

" 'Cause there isn't much to say. But I did call her—like I told you I would. Actually, I was the first one to tell her about what happened to you. She felt miserable."

"She did? What'd she say?"

"Well, she didn't say much. But I could tell from her tone that she felt bad. Real bad. But I got to tell you, man, it was like talking to a completely different girl from the one we went out with last weekend. It's like she has a split personality or something. Like in that movie *Sybil* with Sally Fields. Anyhow, after I told her all the gory details about your near-death experience on the lacrosse field, I told her I wanted to talk to her about something else. At first, she said she was busy and had to hang up, but I kept after her, and finally she said I could call her after I saw you tonight, around eleven. As soon as I get home, I'll call her. And do everything I can to convince her to get back together with you. How's that sound?"

Pretty awful. Like the worst possible thing I could ever want to happen. Ricky liked Rachel. I had suspected that before. But now I knew it for sure. I wanted to tell him to forget it, but my brain felt like mush. I wasn't sure what medication the nurse had just given me, but I was willing to bet it was a sleeping pill. I closed my eyes for a minute and when I reopened them, Ricky was gone and my room was black. I looked at the clock beside me. It was 11:15. I dialed Rachel's number. It was busy. I dialed Ricky's number. It was busy. I wondered where my clothes were and if it were possible to sneak out of the room, but before I could climb out of the miserable bed, I was lying on the pillow again, fading back into unconsciousness.

The nurse woke me a million times that night. "It's just to make sure you're not having any ill effects from your concussion," she told me each time she shook me awake from my deep sleep. I wanted to tell her the only ill effects I was having from the concussion was her waking me up every hour, but my lips were too heavy to move. "My heart is in trouble," I also wanted to yell at her. "I think it stopped." But again, I was mute.

A poor, pathetic, almost-strangled, definitely dumped mute. The scene at the field was nothing in comparison to what had happened to me in my hospital room. Murphy and Caruso may have tried to strangle me, but my best friend since nursery school had murdered me.

•13

The next week was totally miserable. I couldn't do one thing right. It was as if I had fallen under a bad cloud and there was no getting out from under it. All it did was rain on me. Day and night.

First of all, my mother was driving me crazy. The scene with Tony and Brian had done a number on her. After she insisted I stay home from school for three days, she spent all her time figuring out ways Sam and I could get hurt and how she could prevent those calamities from happening. For instance, she decided that Ricky was no longer a trustworthy driver, and the only person who could drive me anywhere was her. If my lacrosse practice was over at four, I had to call her from the field and wait until she left the shelter and picked me up. That was not only ridiculous, it was a pain in the neck. It would take her a half hour to get from the shelter to the field and five minutes to drive me home. But she had to do it. Just the way she had to pick up Sam from baseball practice and drive him home rather than let him ride his bicycle. And she wouldn't go out at night with my father and leave me and Sam alone. Like we were babies who still needed baby-sitters. And she went ballistic with the phone. She was the only one who could answer it. It was always for me, but that didn't matter. It gave her the chance to find out who was calling me. If the caller's voice was unfamiliar, he didn't get to talk to me. She'd tell him I was out—without asking his name.

"I'm sorry," she told me when I freaked about her new set of restrictions. "I never understood what danger you and Sam were in because of Daddy's position until this whole thing happened. I was stupid to have assumed we could lead a normal family life. My head was buried in the sand. But it isn't any longer. You were almost strangled by someone because of Daddy's work. I'm not going to ignore that."

My father tried to talk to her, but she was furious with him. I'd never seen her so mad at him. She answered his questions when he talked to her, but other than that, she had nothing to say to him. I hated seeing the two of them like that. "Just give her some time," my dad said. "I know her better than you do. In a week, she'll be her normal self and you'll be cooking your own dinner and begging rides to school."

I might have been able to cope with my mother's weird behavior if my own life hadn't been so out of sync. Especially with lacrosse. I was a total loser behind the net. All my normal instincts were screwed up. When I'd assume an offense man was coming to my right, he'd appear on my left. The guy I picked to get the ball never did. But the one I wasn't concerned about scored on me. A ball I was sure was aiming for my stomach sailed over my right shoulder. I'd stoop down to get ready to cradle the ball and it would whiz past my head. I was a sitting duck. Ipswich scored eleven goals against me, all eleven of which were my fault—balls I should have scooped up with my stick. In the middle of a game against Rockville, Coach Wetherbee brought in Chip Norris to replace me after I'd given up seven goals in the first quarter. Chip only gave up one more goal during the rest of the game but we lost 8-7. Coach was cool, telling me I hadn't recovered from my concussion. But that wasn't true. Dr. Sontz had given me permission to play. All I knew was that without my success on the lacrosse field, I felt naked. Worthless and dumb and naked. I had never realized until then how much lacrosse meant to me, how much my self-esteem relied on my victories in the net.

My teammates didn't mean to be cruel, but it was hard for them to ignore what was happening to me. "You're in a slight slump," Dana told me when Coach Wetherbee took me out of the net against Rockville. "After a rest, you'll be unstoppable again." But I noticed him quietly urging the coach not to put me back in once Chip took over the net.

"It's not your fault," Paul told me in the middle of one horrific period. "It's the rest of us. We're not protecting you." But both of us knew that I never used to need protecting. I was a take-charge goalie; I let my teammates concentrate on scoring. We played a different kind of game when I was in top form. I was demoralizing the team with my ineptitude.

Academically, I wasn't much better. I couldn't concentrate on any of my classes. I wrote a paper on Miller's *All My Sons* that Mr. Braunstein gave me back with the comment, "This does not even begin to compare with your usual work. Try again." But I didn't. When he asked me about my paper, I shrugged and told him he'd have to grade me on the original paper. He did. I got a D, the first in my life. "And that's being generous," he told me when he handed me back the paper. I also flunked a math test and cut a French class when we were having a quiz.

As if it weren't enough that I was falling apart on the lacrosse field and in my classes and my mother had flipped out, my best friend was finishing me off. Ricky Berg, my best friend since we were three years old and sat next to each other in the sandbox of our nursery school, was chasing my girl. "I'm getting through to her, man," he assured me after the first time I saw them together at Rachel's locker. It was weird. I'd liked her all right when we were hanging out together, but as soon as she'd turned me off, I liked her even more. "I'll have the two of you back together in no time flat."

Apparently, it was taking a little more time than he thought, since this getting together business seemed to require him to drive her to and from school and to take her out for a couple of sodas and even for pizza one night after her soccer game. It was nice of my buddy to do all this for me. To sacrifice his relationship with old Patsy for my sake. To give up so much of his time and energy to help me out. And, of course, I was grateful. So grateful I would have hired Tony Caruso to do a better job on Ricky than he had done on me if only Caruso wasn't spending a little time in the Department of Youth Services. I probably just should have told Ricky to butt out, but I never had the chance to say a thing to him. Thanks to his full-time job of getting me and Rachel back together, he barely had time for his tennis games and homework. I found it less painful to ignore him every time I saw him and Rachel together than to confront him.

Pam Rogers was a lifesaver. She came up to me the day after my "accident" and told me how glad she was I hadn't been hurt. It was a relief to have her talk to me. Now, every time we passed each other in the corridor, she went out of her way to smile at me and say something nice. Since Rachel went out of her way to ignore me, it felt good to be treated nicely by an attractive female. I wasn't ready to start going out with Pam again. I was pretty sure she wasn't ready for that either. But I was grateful for a smile and a kind word. For that week, that was a big deal.

My father wasn't having such a great week either. Brian's arraignment had to be postponed because his uncle got sick. Tony Caruso turned out to have a criminal record—he'd been arrested for shoplifting twice. He had violated the terms of his probation, and it looked as if he was going to be in the custody of DYS for a long while. It was uncertain whether we would actually go to trial in my case, but my father was disturbed by everything that had to do with both Tony and Brian. "There's more going on here than I can understand," he kept saying. I couldn't help it, but I wasn't all that interested in the whole legal scene. Nothing got me all that interested. Except, perhaps, what was happening between my best friend and my former girlfriend.

At the end of that week, I got a phone call that captured my interest but good. Beth Levine, Brian Murphy's former girlfriend, called and asked if we could meet somewhere soon. "You don't know me," she told me, "but I know you. I don't know who else to talk to, but I have a feeling you're the right person."

The way things were going in my life, I would have met with a serial killer if he could have helped me turn things around. Beth Levine sounded like a safer alternative. Since she had her own car, I managed to sneak out of my house while my mother was watching TV and meet Beth at the corner of my street. She was driving a brand-new black Mitsubishi Eclipse, and she was prettier than the car. She had long black hair like Rachel, but she didn't wear it in a braid. But there was something about Beth that reminded me of Rachel, and whatever it was, it sped up my heartbeat. Beth was older than I was and kind of sophisticated, but I felt comfortable the minute I seated myself in the passenger seat of her car.

"I really appreciate your meeting me on the spur of the moment like this," she told me, shaking my hand vigorously and acting like we'd been friends for years. "I just had to talk to you."

"No problem," I told her. "I have to tell you I was curious about Brian Murphy's girlfriend."

She sighed deeply, offered me a sad smile, and headed her car in the direction of the reservoir, a quiet spot where we'd decided to have our little chat. "I don't know where to begin," she said, when she pulled her car into a space at the edge of the reservoir.

"Tell me about you and Brian," I offered. I felt so at ease with this girl, despite her beauty. It was funny, but I felt as if we had met before or maybe could have been relatives. She seemed warm and likable and unaffected by her good looks.

"Okay," she said. "Here goes. Brian and I dated for about a year. I'm a junior, but that doesn't matter. My parents weren't happy about our dating. My father's president of the temple and he goes crazy if I go out with non-Jewish boys. But Brian really tried to please him. He'd talk to him about sporting events and was super polite. He even got him tickets to the U.S. Open 'cause he knew my dad likes tennis. But he couldn't get anywhere. Finally, Brian and I had to sneak out to see each other. But after about six months, all that got too much for me. I really like Brian. He's fun and good-looking and wicked smart and we have a great time together. But my parents were making me crazy. I swear, they always knew when I snuck out to be with Brian. So I told him we had to break up for a while. I promised I'd work on my parents, but the two of us had to take a break.

"Well, he went nuts. He was like a different guy.

He told me I couldn't dump him like that. That no one ever dumped Brian Murphy. I got scared. So, I did a stupid thing. I told my father. He called Brian's father, and can you believe the two of them got into this shouting match? They said gross things to each other. My mother and I sat there stunned while they screamed. And the next day the temple was defaced."

"Have you talked to the district attorney's office?" I asked her.

"Yes," she answered. "I told them everything I told you. Except for one other little thing."

"What's that?" I asked.

"This is hard for me to tell," she said, and she sat there silently staring out of the windshield of her car for a minute or so. "Okay. I've got to tell someone. I really like Brian. Even though he got so angry when I told him we had to break up. In a way, I can't completely blame him for what he said. I mean, I pretty much dumped him, and that wasn't fair. But there's no way I can believe he did this to the temple. I'm telling you something I can't tell another human being. And you can't repeat it to your father." She was getting so agitated now, it was making me nervous. She looked ready to cry.

I reached across the seat and touched her arm. "I promise you that whatever you tell me will never leave this car," I said. And I meant it. I felt a stronger connection with this girl with every word she spoke. If she had asked me to shave my head in order to prove my loyalty to her, I just might have done it on the spot. And considering my fetish about my hair and Rachel's hatred of shaved heads, that was saying quite a lot.

She sighed deeply before continuing. "I don't think Brian did it alone. Everyone says it's his handwriting. But I'm not so sure. I know he hated my father enough to do it. But someone else had to have helped him."

"That's possible," I agreed. "Who might that have been? Tony Caruso?"

"Oh, definitely not him." Beth's face screwed up in a look of disgust. "I know all about what happened with you and Tony and Brian, but I'm sure that Tony didn't help him."

"I don't see how you can be so sure. To me, it makes sense."

"Well, believe me, it doesn't," she said. "Tony's a thug. I could never understand how Brian hung around with him. I think Brian felt bad for Tony, felt he got a raw deal in life. You know, he never knew his father and his mother's an alcoholic and his brother went to jail for selling drugs. He's not your typical Rockville kid. Brian's a funny guy. He could really care about people. That's why he went so wild when we broke up. I still can't completely understand it. It's not Brian. None of this is. As for Tony, though, he'd never know enough about the concentration camps to have done that."

I had the feeling Beth was not telling me everything she knew. She'd seemed so open before, but now she was clamming up. I wanted to know about Brian, and even though she was talking about him, it was sounding too polished, like she'd rehearsed these words. They didn't sound sincere, the way her words had sounded at the beginning of our talk. Plus, I was all confused about whether she thought Brian had written the words himself or had someone else help him. I hated to let this happen. I had felt so close to getting information I wanted and which I knew she had within her reach. "Beth, please, be honest with me," I said. "I've got a lot at stake here. And it's not just because of my father. I'm involved with this case as much as you. It's affecting my whole life. If you know something else, please tell me. I promise not to tell my father. Or anyone. I just need to know."

Beth looked miserable. "I think it was his mother," she finally said in a soft voice.

"His mother?" I practically shouted back at her. I knew it was important that I keep cool and not push the poor girl away from me with my emotional outburst, but I couldn't contain myself. "He did that with his mother's help?"

"Oh, God," Beth said, hiding her face in her hands. "I don't know anything."

I waited for a few minutes while Beth sat there, leaning against the wheel, her face hidden in her hands. I couldn't think of anything to say to comfort her. Finally, she looked up at me, biting back tears, and said, "I'm as confused as you are, Zack. It's just that I know Brian and his mother are wicked close and he told me she hated me for breaking up with him. I ran into her at the Rockville mall two days ago, and the look she gave me could have killed me on the spot. It's funny, but when Brian and I were going together, it was my parents who opposed it the most. His parents said very little. Or, at least, that's what I thought. They weren't real nice to me when I called Brian, but they were never rude or nasty. But now I think they were as much against our dating as my parents. Only Brian never let on. I mean, we hardly ever went to his house, so how would I know what they were thinking? But after I saw his mom at the mall, I started thinking about it, and it made sense. I can't prove it. It's just a feeling I have. You're the only one I'm telling and I don't even know why I'm telling you. I mean, what can you do? I was so amazed with that story about how you stood up to Tony and Brian at the baseball field and I know your father is the D.A., so I told you."

"Lacrosse field," I said.

''Lacrosse field?'' she repeated.

''Yeah,'' I said. ''It happened at the lacrosse field.''

''Oh, of course,'' she said. ''I should have remembered. I was there when Rockville played Bromley last year and you were awesome against Brian. He respects your ability. But he said he'd get you next time you played. I guess he can't play now. Not with this whole mess going on. You have to feel sort of sorry for the poor kid, don't you? I mean, it's terrible if he actually ends up going to jail for scribbling a few words.''

Up until her last statement, I'd been really caring about this girl. Man, she was pretty. And kind of fragile. I could feel myself starting to fall for her. But her last sentence stopped me cold. ''No, I don't feel the least bit sorry for him,'' I said. All I could see in front of me was Tony Caruso's face as he called me a ''Jewish scum bag.'' The hate had filled every pore of his skin. It was etched into the veins that popped on his neck as he went for mine. That kind of hate wasn't limited to one kid. It had to be stopped. Sure, he'd had a tough life, but that didn't give him the right to attack me because I was Jewish. Maybe sending Brian Murphy to jail wouldn't end all that hate, but it would show people that it's against the law to spread messages of hate like that. I'm not a lawyer and I don't understand what the law says about graffiti, but I knew that Beth Levine was wrong. She was excusing behavior that shouldn't be excused. I was sorry her boyfriend might go to jail. But if he didn't, what was to prevent people from drawing swastikas on every temple in America? For some reason, it scared me more that Beth Levine was excusing Brian Murphy's behavior than it had when Tony Caruso did.

Beth sat up straight in her seat. ''You can't sympathize a little bit with a kid who does something awful because his girlfriend's broken up with him?'' she asked me.

''My girlfriend broke up with me,'' I told her, although I had no idea why I was saying that. ''But I didn't go out and deface a temple with anti-Semitic graffiti, did I?''

''Your girlfriend broke up with you?'' she repeated.

''Yes,'' I said. ''And I'm sure it wasn't any easier for me than for Brian.''

''Had you gone with her for a long time?'' she asked.

''Long enough,'' I said. I wanted to change the subject but I didn't know how. It had been such a stupid thing to have brought it up in the first place. ''Brian did a terrible thing,'' I continued, anxious to get away from the topic of Rachel. ''I don't know whether or not you know this but the Supreme Court recently handed down some new rulings on hate crimes. They upheld the constitutionality of a Wisconsin law that lengthens prison sentences and raises fines in criminal cases where the guilty party is found to have chosen the victim for his race, religion, or color. The court wants to punish hate crimes like the one your ex-boyfriend committed at your temple.''

Beth didn't seem to be hearing my diatribe on the law. Actually, I couldn't believe I remembered that stuff about Wisconsin. I'd read it in a newspaper article my father had left on my desk that morning. She seemed to be looking right through me. ''That's interesting,'' she said, ''but I'm more interested in your girlfriend. She's the one with the long black braid, isn't she?''

''Yes,'' I said. ''How did you know that?''

''I noticed her at the Rockville game. She was standing on the Bromley side, screaming out your name. She and some woman with a huge sheepdog that barked a lot.'' I nodded. ''She's beautiful,'' Beth continued, ''really beautiful. I'm sorry she split. It must be hard for you."

"Look, I've really got to get home," I said. I was beginning to sweat. "I've got a lot of homework to do."

"Oh, sure, I understand," Beth said, starting her car's engine. "I just hope everything I told you will be kept in the strictest confidence."

"I gave you my word," I said.

Beth kept talking about how pretty my ex-girlfriend was until we got to my street. "You know, I could be all wrong about Brian's mom," she said when I started to get out of the car. "I'm so out of it over this whole thing, I don't know what's going on. You know, my folks aren't exactly looking forward to the publicity when the whole story hits the newspapers. Just imagine how it's going to sound when they write about the boyfriend of the daughter of the president of the temple who defaced the temple."

"It'll sound awful," I agreed.

She shook her head. I wanted to dislike this girl, but she was making it hard. She reached over and took my hand before I was out of the car. "Please don't think I'm a total loser," she said sincerely. "I'm still reeling over this whole thing. You know how you feel about your girlfriend? Well, I feel the same way about Brian. My feelings are real complicated. You're the first person I could talk to honestly about it all. I'm sure it would have been a lot better for me if I'd lied to you, but I just chose you as the one person I could speak the truth to. That's a lot of responsibility for some poor guy who doesn't even know me."

"No problem," I said. "Your story's safe with me." I was beginning to wonder if the whole world was filled with people with multiple personalities like Brian Murphy and Beth Levine. Or maybe those types were just attracted to me.

"And yours, too," she said, releasing my hand. "But I've got to tell you, your girlfriend, Robin, she's the loser."

"Rachel," I muttered as I closed the passenger door behind me and walked toward my house.

14

It wasn't easy but after school the next day, I foiled my mother's protective custody screen and took the bus to Rockville. It left me off two blocks from Temple Israel. I wasn't certain why I felt the need to go to the temple, but from the minute I'd left Beth Levine's car, I needed to see the graffiti for myself. I'd never been to Temple Israel before, and although I'd seen plenty of graffiti on walls and in public bathrooms, I'd never seen any anti-Semitic graffiti. But I knew it was about time I saw for myself exactly what it was that had turned my life into such a confusing mess.

Temple Israel was situated at the top of a hill in a nice section of Rockville. It was kind of a big temple, at least bigger than Temple Beth-El, the temple in Bromley where I was bar mitzvahed a few years earlier. It was an all-brick building, unlike Temple Beth-El which was pretty much a wooden structure. It was funny, but when I first saw all the brick, all I could think about was the Three Little Pigs. I could imagine the big bad wolf, huffing and puffing to blow the house down. For a minute, I wished Temple Beth-El were also made of bricks, but, at least, I reminded myself, it wasn't made of straw. I was feeling kind of silly, standing there in front of this big brick building, thinking about a children's story, but it was better than thinking about Brian Murphy standing here, hating this building and all its members so badly that he wanted to hurt them in any way he could.

After a few minutes of letting my mind go wild, I walked up to the front door and looked at the graffiti. My father had told me that the police wanted to wash it off, but the rabbi of the Temple Israel had decided to let it stay for a while, as a lesson to anyone who came to look at it. I wasn't sure I agreed with that. After all, the only people who would come to this temple were Jews who would be upset by the graffiti. But my father agreed with the rabbi. He said it showed courage to try to teach people that these kinds of words constitute a hate crime. They can be erased, and will be, he said, but we all need to see for ourselves how evil they are and how much they hurt innocent people. In a way, the rabbi and my dad were right and I was wrong, for here I was. I'd come to see the words and try to understand exactly what a hate crime was.

The first thing I noticed when I looked at the graffiti was how neatly it was all written. It was as if whoever had written it had had all the time in the world. Each letter was carefully and neatly drawn. The paint was black and it showed up clearly against the white front door of the temple. First there were the names of the seven camps, all in capital letters: AUSCHWITZ, AUSCHWITZ-BIRKENAU, MAJDANEK, CHELMNO, TREBLINKA, BELZEC, SOBIBOR. There was even a little dot over the "z" in Belzec and a slash mark over the second "o" in Sobibor. It hurt to look at those names, so neatly and clearly etched in black paint upon that front door. They seemed more offensive than the grossest swear words I could imagine.

I stared at those seven names for a long time. They

grew uglier and scarier each second I studied them. That morning, before I left for school, I had read a few things about the concentration camps in some sheets I'd found inside my Hebrew school books. My Hebrew school history books actually say little about the Holocaust, but a speaker from this special educational program called "Facing History and Ourselves" had given us a lot of information about the Holocaust. I'd never even looked at the sheets till that morning. The camp names Brian had written on the temple door were all death camps. Sobibor had been put out of business by the underground when some Russian prisoners of war were sent there and organized an uprising. There were many other camps. Something like six hundred subcamps, or camps within camps. I'd have to reread the sheets when I got home.

Slowly, I let my eyes move from this list of names to the words beneath it. "Don't Buy From Jews," "Germans Defend Yourselves," "Long Live Hitler." That was it. Just those three little phrases. The first two phrases I recognized from my "Facing History" sheets. Germans had written those words on the doors of Jewish businesses as part of a boycott against Jewish businessmen during Hitler's rise to power in the late 1930s. How had Brian gotten that information? Maybe a speaker from "Facing History" had come to Rockville High. Like me, Brian must have saved the sheets. Incredible. Sick, but incredible.

I stood there for a long time and reread each word painted on the temple door. It hurt every time I looked at each word. It hurt just as bad as when Rachel had dumped me. I wished I had some white paint with me so I could obliterate those loathsome words. Why should anyone else have to read them and be sickened? Especially anyone who had survived the Holocaust or lost loved ones during that heinous time. More than that, however, I wanted to take the biggest rock I could find and hurl it at Brian Murphy's head. It took a while, but those feelings finally began to go away. The rabbi and my father were right. It was important that people see how harmful these words were to every American's freedom. And I didn't want to kill anybody. But I did want to be certain that whoever did this terrible thing paid for his crime. I wanted to say a prayer before I left the temple, but I couldn't think of anything except the blessing over the wine, so I said that.

I could hardly wait for Brian's trial to begin. The day of Brian's arraignment, my father seemed confident. "I can't say I'm totally pleased with the way things are going with this case," he told me at breakfast. "I'm still in the dark about a lot of things I should know. But I am certain Brian committed the crime and I know the judge will arraign him today. What else I'm certain about is his defense. It's going to be strong. His uncle's a good lawyer. It should be an interesting trial, to say the least."

My mother was more relaxed that morning. We had heard the night before from Tony's court-appointed lawyer that he was pleading guilty to the assault charges and that there would be no trial for him for that crime, anyhow. Whether Brian would be tried as an accessory seemed unlikely, but my mother was cool about that. She agreed to let Ricky pick me up and told Sam he could ride his bike to school. She even seemed more interested in the yellow-and-white kitten she'd brought home from the shelter the night before than she did about my plans for getting home from lacrosse practice. I knew she'd gone for a long jog with my father before breakfast and he must have said the right things to calm her down. I had to give the guy credit. He'd performed a minor miracle.

Personally, I, too, was struggling to get my life back in order. I'd studied for my math quiz and done an extra credit paper for lit. Mr. Braunstein seemed pleased with my effort. I'd had a long conversation with Pam the night before and had hung up feeling pretty good. We weren't going out or anything like that, but we were turning into good friends. I was glad that a girl I'd once gone out with and broken up with could end up my friend. We'd even discussed Rachel. "She's strange," Pam had said. "I don't know her real well, but she's in my gym class and we've talked a few times. She's kind of spacey, like sometimes she's there and sometimes she isn't."

"Maybe that's because of me," I said. "I mean, it might be hard for her to be open with you because of me."

"No, that's not it," she said. "I've seen her with other people. Sometimes she's real friendly. But other times, she clams right up. Like she doesn't know you at all. I know she and Diane Halpert are best friends and Diane's a great kid, but I can't get a handle on Rachel. I have a cousin like that. It drives me crazy. I never know how she's going to act."

I thought about Pam's words a lot. After all, she could "get a handle" on just about everybody. Rachel had usually been upbeat with me. But I'd seen the way she acted around her mother sometimes, and she could be moody. Still, none of that mattered. Moodiness, I could live with. It wasn't such a big deal. I would have done anything to get her back. I couldn't pass her in the school corridor or think about her in my room without feeling awful. It didn't seem possible we were history.

"Man, you're not history at all," Ricky insisted when I cornered him at the tennis court. He was warming up for a tennis match and I knew it wasn't fair to bother him right before a match, but I wasn't having any luck bothering him during the school day. I was certain he was avoiding me. And why not? He'd stolen my girlfriend under the guise of helping me get back together with her. He was right to avoid me. Just seeing him standing there in his spiffy red, black, and white school tennis outfit enraged me. I wanted to shove his tennis racket down his throat. Instead, I stood there, waiting patiently for whatever crumbs of hope that throat might offer me. "Rachel's getting ready to talk to you herself."

"Are you serious?" I asked. Suddenly, he was my best friend again. It was amazing how quickly I could switch from hating this kid to fawning all over him. Maybe the run-in at the lacrosse field with Tony had damaged my brain. "When?"

"Oh, real soon. Maybe tonight. You going to be home?"

"Where else would I be?"

"Oh, I don't know," he said, "maybe hanging around with old Pamela."

"Pam?" I said. "Are you nuts? I'm not taking her out."

"Really? 'Cause it looked that way when I saw you two at your locker this morning."

I remembered that scene. Pam had been showing me a picture of the two of us that she'd found in her locker. It was a photo of the two of us dressed up like a hot dog and a roll for a costume party. Pam was wicked creative. She'd made the costumes. I really did look like a hot dog roll smeared with mustard, and she was a dead ringer for a plump juicy hot dog. Just as we were laughing ourselves silly over that picture, who walked by but Rachel and Ricky. Just as happy as any couple could look. I'd gotten so angry at the sight of the two of them together that I'd gone out of my way to continue laughing with Pam. I'd derived some sick sense of satisfaction from knowing the two of them had seen us laughing together. Of course, the minute they walked out of our view, I'd become so depressed I'd dropped the photograph on the floor. "Yeah, well, we're not dating," I repeated.

"Sure. Cool, man. Whatever you say," Ricky said as his opponent approached the court. "I gotta go now. Later."

I could have stayed to watch some of his match. My lacrosse practice wasn't starting for a half hour. But his opponent looked like a loser and the last thing I wanted was to see Ricky win a match. Instead, I went to my own lacrosse practice and did so poorly Coach Wetherbee blasted me in front of the whole team. I couldn't blame him. I was missing every shot that came to me. All I wanted to do was throw down my stick and walk on out of there. Quit right on the spot. But I couldn't do that. Lacrosse was about the only thing I had going for me. And Sam didn't need to have a brother who quit when the going got rough. I couldn't give up. Not yet, anyhow. But I knew there was one thing I did have to do. The second practice ended. I threw my equipment into my locker and walked—no, ran—to Rachel's house. Ricky had told me she was getting ready to call me that evening. But that evening was a long way off. If losing Rachel for good was my fate, fine. So be it. But, damn it all, I had to know why.

Mrs. Levy turned all red when she opened the door and saw me, sweaty and red in the face myself, standing there. "Rachel's not here," she told me, but I knew she was lying.

"Yes, she is," I insisted. "I can hear her music coming from upstairs. Please, Mrs. Levy, just let me go talk to her."

"I can't do that, Zack," she said and looked like she

was going to cry. "Please don't bother her now. Maybe in a few days."

"I don't have a few days," I pleaded. "I'll only stay a few minutes. I just have to ask her a few questions."

"Questions," Mrs. Levy repeated. "That's all your friend, that Ricky boy, asks. Questions and more questions. My poor Rachel's being asked too many questions. I don't want her to be hurt by all you boys and your questions." Her voice was rising with each word. "Please, just go. I won't let you see my daughter! Just go home!"

I was stunned. Mrs. Levy was shouting at me. I wouldn't have believed that I could feel any worse, but I did. What choice did I have but to leave? I had turned to go when I heard Rachel's voice. "Please, Mama," she was saying. "Don't be upset. I'll talk to him and take care of it."

I turned back around to see Rachel standing beside her mother. Mrs. Levy sighed deeply and walked into her kitchen. "Let's go to my room for a few minutes," Rachel said to me, and I followed obediently.

"I'm sorry, Rachel," I said when she sat down on her bed and patted a spot beside her for me. "I had no idea I would upset your mother so much. I'm so confused I don't know what to say."

"There's nothing you can say," she said as she shook her head back and forth. She looked tired but as beautiful as ever. She was not as agitated as her mother, but she was upset. "Please, let me try and explain what's happening here," she began, speaking slowly and clearly as if she were telling a story to a small child. "I tried to explain it to Ricky and I think he understands, but you're the one I should have been talking to, not your best friend." I nodded.

"Here goes," she continued in the same teacherish voice. "Zack, I should have told you all this when we met, but I didn't. That was my mistake. My parents are both survivors. Concentration camp survivors. My mother spent two years at Auschwitz, and my father endured two years at Buchenwald and three at Auschwitz. My mother was ten when she and her parents and three older sisters were taken to Auschwitz. My father was eleven when he left for Buchenwald. What saved them was that they both looked older. And they were in excellent health. My mother passed for sixteen and my father for an eighteen-year-old. She was very pretty, and he was strong and able to work hard. Both their parents and two of my mother's sisters and my father's sister and brother perished at the concentration camps the day they arrived. Not one of the eight of them made it through the first selection.

"My mother's sister had the job of making lists of the numbers tattooed on the arms of the bodies after they were gassed in the showers. The Germans were meticulous in their record keeping. They wanted to account for every Jew they murdered. My mother's sister was very good at her work. She protected my mother in every way possible and had my mother help her with her job. One day my mother recognized her aunt's and her two cousins' bodies. Still my mother did her job. She also worked for Eichmann once he came to Auschwitz. That day, she served him lunch while he watched a mass execution. She later learned that her sister was killed in that execution. Eichmann asked her to make him another sandwich in the middle of it. When he was on trial in Israel, she was called as a witness. She traveled to Israel and testified about the mass execution. She witnessed his execution. My father worked in the fields. He only slept four hours a night, but he never stopped working.

"Unspeakable horrors happened to each of them in the camps, but they survived. They were liberated by the Russians. They were the only ones in all of their large extended families to survive. They met in the German displaced persons camp where they were sent after the war. My mother wasn't even thirteen then, but they married in the camp four years later. They both wanted to go to America, but they couldn't for another year because of the immigration laws. My mother had a baby in the displaced persons camp outside of Munich. He died of dysentery. She never expected to have another child, but I was born in New York when she was forty-seven years old.

"You must understand that I was raised by parents who never felt the world could be safe again for Jews. My mother came to America when she was nineteen. She was terrified of the dark, of strangers, of loud noises, of flying, of animals, of being in crowds, and of being alone. She suffered from migraines and colitis. My father had tuberculosis and was in a sanatorium for a year after they came to New York. But he's a lot stronger than my mother. He found an escape in literature and religion that my mother never shared.

"This is the heritage my parents left. They tried not to pass it on to me, but how could they not? They tried to make me feel safe, safer than they were ever able to feel, but they couldn't do that. I inhaled their fears along with their love and attention. I inherited these fears the way I inherited my father's black hair and my mother's blue eyes. How could I not?

"And why am I telling you all this? Because it's part of me. I try to hide it, to appear cheerful and happy, and I can do that most of the time. When you told me about the graffiti, I was okay. For a while. But then when you told me about Brian Murphy and Tony Marino, I began to have nightmares. Nightmares about places I've never seen, places where my parents were sent. Nightmares about shaved heads and emaciated bodies. I'm sorry, Zack. But I'm different. It's not my fault I'm this way. That much, I do understand. It's society's, whoever they are. Society allowed the Holocaust to happen. It allowed six million Jews to be murdered. It allowed my parents and their families to endure unspeakable horrors. There is so much I don't understand, no matter how hard I try. But there is no way I can deny the fact that my life has been shaped by what happened to my parents almost fifty years ago. I want so much to be perfect and happy, to give my parents the pleasure they were denied. But I'm not. And the harder I try to be that way, the more I fail. Just the way I failed you. You want a happy, cheerful Rachel, and I want to give you one, but sometimes, I just can't find that person."

I heard her words, her long, sad story as if I were sitting in an auditorium at school, listening to a teacher give a lecture. My God, I'd seen the name of one of the concentration camps she'd mentioned painted on the door of Temple Israel. To think Mr. and Mrs. Levy were survivors. I'd actually met a survivor from one of the camps before. She'd come to our school last year to tell us about her personal experiences in Buchenwald. Her name was Sonia Weitz, and she was a pretty woman with black hair pulled back into a neat ball at the back of her neck. The whole time she was telling us about the horrors she endured during her four years in the camp, I kept staring at her hair and wondering how it was possible that someone could survive such atrocities and still have such nice hair. I know I have a hair fetish, but still I had to concentrate on her hair or I could not have digested her words. For a minute, sitting on Rachel's bed, I wondered if Brian Murphy and Tony Caruso had heard Sonia speak at their school. How could they have heard her story and still been so filled with hate for the Jews? None of it made sense.

"I'm sorry, Rachel," I said when I realized that Rachel had finished speaking and was staring at me, waiting for me to say something. There was so much I wanted to say, but the right words wouldn't come. My words seemed so inadequate after what she had just told me. "I'm sorry that I caused you any more pain."

"It wasn't you, Zack," she said. "It's me. I'm the one with the problems."

"We all have problems, Rachel. I have problems. I worry about going bald. I worry about getting lousy grades and being beaten up by anti-Semites. I worry about not being able to catch a lacrosse ball in the crease of my stick ever again. I worry about my parents getting sick and old. I worry about Hamlet rejecting Ophelia. I worry about you not talking to me and running off with my best friend."

Rachel smiled. It was wonderful to see her smile. I knew I was sounding like a total idiot, but if that's what it took to make her smile, it was worth it. "You don't have to worry about me and your best friend," she said. "You're cuter than Ricky. But he is the best listener."

That stung. "I know," I admitted. "He'll make a great shrink someday, won't he?"

She nodded. "And I should know. I've been to enough of them. My parents were smart enough to realize their childhoods affected mine. They made sure I had a wonderful therapist in New York to discuss my fears and worries with. We were in family therapy for six years, and it was painful but helped us all. My mother has come a long way in the past ten years. But since we moved here, I haven't seen anyone, and I guess that's a mistake when you have the problems I have. It helped me to open up to Ricky, to let someone see the sad Rachel. It made me realize how much I've been keeping inside since we moved here."

"I'm glad," I said. "I just wish I could have been the first one to have heard all this, not Ricky."

"I couldn't tell you before. I liked you too much. So I retreated. But Ricky sensed that and he helped me. Please don't be jealous of him. And let me be friends with him."

Man, was she asking a lot. Sharing my girl with Ricky was not going to be easy. There were a lot of things I could share: food, Coke, clothes, and sporting equipment. But Rachel? No way. "Couldn't you just find a new shrink?" I asked. "I'm sure there's lots of good ones in Boston."

"I'm sure there are." She looked a little hurt.

"Not that I think you need one or anything. To me, you're perfect."

She smiled. "Don't worry about it, Zack. I know what my problems are. I'm the child of Holocaust survivors and that puts me in a special category. Things throw me for a loop that wouldn't bother the ordinary person. Ricky said I was fragile and he's right. But I was wrong not to be honest with you. I care for you, Zack. I don't want to lose you."

Her final words were so terrific, I tried not to focus on the mention of Ricky's name before she spoke them. "You haven't lost me," I said. "I want to know everything about you. What makes you happy and what makes you sad." I moved closer to her and put my arms around her. It felt so good to have her body against mine. Slowly, the pain was leaving me and Rachel was filling all my empty spaces. There were so many thoughts crowding my mind, but I pushed them all out of my mind and let in only the pleasure. Rachel was back in my arms, in my life, and nothing else mattered.

15

Man, it was great to have Rachel back. The first thing she wanted to do was visit the shelter. My mother was psyched to see her and immediately led her over to the five six-week-old golden retriever puppies that had been left at the shelter a few days earlier. Rachel went nuts over the puppies. While I was changing dirty papers and washing out cages, Rachel sat on the floor, feeding the five puppies, looking happier than I'd ever seen her.

"It would be cool to give her one of the puppies," I told my mother. "What do you think?"

"You know my philosophy on that subject," she reminded me. "You never give a puppy as a gift to anyone. If you want to surprise someone, give her a necklace or a sweater. Those gifts can be returned. It's heartbreaking to return an animal. If Rachel's parents had wanted her to have a dog, don't you think they would have given her one by now?"

"Yeah," I agreed. "Rachel said her mother used to be afraid of animals. Maybe that was a long time ago. You know, maybe at the concentration camp. How 'bout if I ask her mother? If she says okay, then can we do it?"

"Sounds fine to me," my mom said, looking over at

Rachel and smiling. I'd told my mother all about Rachel's parents, and she'd cried during my story. She'd wanted to call the Levys and invite them over for dinner, but I'd convinced her not to. I couldn't imagine the seven of us having dinner in my house. I was having a hard enough time working out my relationship with this girl without involving my parents. "What a picture she makes with those dogs. Such a pretty girl. I can see why you're crazy about her."

She kissed the top of my head as she walked out of the room. I didn't flinch. I felt so good at that moment I could have kissed Miss London, my math teacher, the homeliest and nastiest woman on the face of this earth. I was excited about the chance to call Mrs. Levy. She had been hesitant about Rachel going off with me that afternoon. I knew she was worried about Rachel and me. It would be nice to have a conversation with her without Rachel around.

"A dog?" she questioned when I'd snuck away from Rachel and called her about the puppies. "Rachel wants a dog now?"

"Well, she hasn't exactly said that," I said, "but you should see her with the golden retriever puppies. You've never seen anybody so happy. My mom said she could adopt one if you approved. She's real fussy about who adopts her puppies, but she thinks Rachel would be fine. We could surprise her with it. If you and Mr. Levy say okay."

"She wanted a dog or a cat in New York," Mrs. Levy told me, "but we were in an apartment and they didn't allow pets. She asked when we moved here, but what do I know about dogs? I'm not as afraid as I used to be when I see them. I told her her father was allergic, but he's not. She hasn't mentioned it in a long time. They're a lot of work, aren't they?"

"Oh, they have to be walked and fed and trained,"

I admitted. "It's hard if everyone in the family works. But you don't, do you?"

"Oh, no. But do you think I could learn how to walk a dog?"

She sounded like a kid herself. "Absolutely," I said. "And I'm sure Rachel could do it before school. I'd be glad to teach the two of you whatever you need to know about caring for a dog."

"Oh, let's try it," she said. "And thank you, Zack. You're a good boy. You and your friend, Ricky Berg. You're both so good to my Rachel."

I nearly gagged. Was it always going to be me and Ricky together in her mind? God, I hoped not. But, still, her approval on this dog business was great.

The best part of the whole thing was surprising Rachel with the dog. It was hard for her to let go of the puppies when it was time for us to leave. After she put each one of them back into his crate, I picked up the one she'd had the hardest time saying good-bye to. "This guy's really crying," I told her. "He's in a bad way."

"Oh, Zack," she moaned, "I feel terrible. It was so selfish of me to play with him so long. The poor baby. He does seem to be crying, doesn't he?"

"He does," I agreed. "And there's only one thing we can do about it."

"What's that?" she asked miserably.

"This," I said as I handed the squirmy ball of yellow fur to her. "You've got to make him yours."

"Mine?" she asked, cradling him against her chest. "How can I make him mine?"

"Easy. Just take him home, train him, feed him, and walk him. And, most of all, love him."

Rachel's eyes opened wide. "Oh, I'd love to," she said, "but my mother would have a fit. Remember.

She's afraid of dogs. And she always told me my father's allergic."

"No, she's not," I said, "and he's not either."

Suddenly, Rachel understood. "You talked to her!" she screamed.

I nodded.

"She said yes!"

I nodded again.

"And your mom said yes!"

One more nod from the big guy, and she and the puppy were pushing themselves against my chest. "I'm calling him 'Lax,' 'cause he's coming to every one of your lacrosse games," she told me, and my heart sank because I wasn't sure I was going to be playing in any more lacrosse games.

As it turned out, however, Lax brought me good luck. As quickly as it had vanished, my skill before the net returned. It was as if the ball and I had finally gotten back in sync with one another. It took a turn to the right, and my stick was there to retrieve it. It bounced to the left, and I had it in my crease before it hit the ground. I was flying all over the place and never came up empty. Always the ball was safely in my clutches. My teammates went nuts. Twice during a game against Morrisville, they rushed me, picking me up and hugging me like madmen. "I love you, baby!" Dana Kessel kept screaming into my face every time I made a save.

It was funny, but as thrilled as I was with my performances, I couldn't forget the frustration of playing poorly. It was as if I had hit rock bottom and was now floating on top of the world. But I was different. Now I realized how fleeting glory was. Yes, I was playing well at that moment and everyone on my team loved me. But that love was conditional on my success at the net. So long as I came up with the ball, I was a hero.

When I missed it, game after game, practice after practice, I was a loser. As much as I loved the sport of lacrosse, I couldn't imagine anyone throwing his whole life into any sport where success was so slippery.

My father's career, however, didn't seem much more appetizing. The case against Brian Murphy was going worse than he had expected. "I'm not sure what we're up against here," he told my mom and me while he was getting supper ready after my game against Morrisville. "We have handwriting analysts able to prove it was Brian's handwriting on the temple. We have his fingerprints all over the door. We even have a witness who saw him leaving the temple grounds with a can of paint the night of the incident. Yet his uncle is trying to plea-bargain, claiming there are extenuating circumstances, winning delays without revealing any information. Saul Serben is the judge, and he's as confused as I am. He's an exceptionally sympathetic and fair judge, but even his patience is being tested to the max. Today, I was supposed to sit down with John Donahue, Brian's uncle, but at the last moment he didn't show up. Tomorrow, either he lets us know what's going on or we go right to trial, whether he's ready or not. He's making us look like fools and I'm not at all sure how he's doing it."

"It sounds like you're letting him get away with an awful lot," my mother said. She was boiling some rice and hamburger for a chocolate lab with a queasy stomach. "That's not like you."

"You're right," he admitted, "but his uncle is quite persuasive. He's pretty close to his nephew and very disturbed about the whole case. I don't know what it is, but when we sit down, I'm putty in his hands."

"That doesn't sound like you, Dad," I added. My father was known as a tough but fair prosecutor. "I hope it doesn't have anything to do with what happened between me and those guys."

"It doesn't," my father insisted. "It's the missing element. Patty agrees. She's baffled too, and that doesn't happen often. But don't worry. Tomorrow, Donahue and I appear in Serben's office, and this case begins in earnest."

After dinner, I went over to Rachel's to help her walk Lax and wasn't happy to find my good buddy Ricky already there.

"I just had to see this little guy for myself," he greeted me. He was sitting on the floor of the Levy kitchen right next to Rachel, and Lax was jumping all over him. Just the way he had jumped all over me at the field after my game. Mrs. Levy was pulling a pan of butterscotch brownies out of the oven. Ricky's favorite dessert. My first impulse upon walking in on this happy scene was to turn around and walk out. That would show Rachel how I felt about her relationship with my supposed best friend. My next impulse was to flatten Ricky, but since that was the impulse I experienced every time I saw the little runt lately, I was experienced in squashing it. So I smiled at everyone gathered in the Levy kitchen, snatched a brownie out of the hot pan without scorching my hand, and fastened Lax's leash to his collar. Five minutes later, Ricky, Rachel, and I were walking Lax down Rachel's street.

"Heard you had a great game against Morrisville today, buddy," Ricky said, thumping me on the back like a real jock.

"He was dynamite," Rachel said. "Poor Morrisville didn't stand a chance against this big guy."

"I was hot," I admitted. "Since I was cold for a good week, it was a nice change."

"I intend to make sure he stays hot for the rest of the season," Rachel said. She'd never looked prettier or sounded crazier over me. "Heard you had a great game today, too," she said to Ricky, and I felt my body tighten. I was a balloon. One minute, Rachel was blowing air into me and the next minute she was squeezing it out. Life around her was a roller-coaster ride.

"Oh, you did, huh?" Ricky said. "And how did you hear that since you were all the way in Morrisville watching a lacrosse game?"

"Oh, I have spies," she said, and she gave him a big smile. Man, did it hurt to see her smiling like that at Ricky. There I was, heading for deflation again.

"Yeah, I played okay," Ricky answered her, so humble he made me sick. "Tomorrow's a rough game against Lancaster. I could use a cheering squad for that one, in case you guys are around."

Be still, hands, I told myself as I struggled not to punch out his lights.

"We'll see," Rachel answered sweetly, and I wondered if this was all part of a plot to make me lose my mind. If so, it was working perfectly.

"So, what's going on with the Murphy case?" Ricky asked me.

It caught me by surprise, his mentioning the case in front of Rachel. I wasn't anxious to bring up the subject that had caused her all that grief. I glanced at her face and saw nothing but pleasure. Great. He knew Rachel better than me. "It's not going so great," I said. "I can't tell you any details—not that I know them—but I know it's not all working out as smoothly as my father had hoped."

"I saw Brian Murphy today," Rachel said, "at your lacrosse game, Zack. He was there with a couple of other guys from his team. Well, they all had Rockville Lacrosse on their jackets, anyhow."

"No kidding," I said. "I didn't notice any of them."

"Well, you were sort of busy," she said. "Do you

think it's that unusual for them to show up at a Bromley-Morrisville game?''

''Yeah, sort of,'' I said. ''It's not like it was a big game or anything.''

''Sounds strange to me,'' Ricky agreed. ''How did they act during the game, Rachel?''

''I didn't see them until the end,'' she said. ''Diane noticed them first. She said they were staring at me from the minute we arrived. It must have been Lax they were looking at. He's so cute.''

She sounded fine, but I was getting nervous. And I didn't know why. ''How many of them were at the game?'' I asked.

''Four guys with the jackets, including Brian,'' she said. ''And one girl. Diane said her name was Beth Levine. I'd never seen Brian before. Diane pointed him out. It was hard looking at him and not saying anything to him.''

''I'm sure it was,'' Ricky said in his shrinky voice, real low and steady. ''I wish I'd been there.''

I couldn't just let that go by. ''Oh, yeah,'' I blurted out, ''and what would you have done? I mean, I wasn't there for you to hide behind.''

It was a lousy thing to say, and I knew it. But this conversation was driving me crazy. I was a balloon, stretched and deflated way too often. My elasticity was shot to hell.

But Ricky was in perfect control. ''I admit I wasn't feeling too brave when I wandered into that Caruso house. You're right. I would have ended up hamburger at the game.''

The look Rachel gave me wasn't filled with hate. But it sure wasn't filled with the same affection she'd offered me at the beginning of the walk. I felt like a crumb. ''Oh, I know how that feels, all right,'' I said.

''I just wonder what they were doing there,'' Ricky

repeated, having won this round without having had to throw one punch. "I don't like the feel of this whole thing."

"Maybe I should have said something to your coach," Rachel said to me. "I didn't think about it much until now."

"Don't worry," I said. "There was nothing he could have done. It's not against the law for a team to watch one of our games. I'm curious about Beth Levine. You remember her, don't you, Ricky? Brian's Jewish girlfriend."

"Oh, yeah," Ricky said. "I remember that conversation about her in Caruso's house. What does she look like?"

"She's good-looking," I said, without thinking. "Long black hair."

They both looked at me like I'd said I'd robbed a bank and murdered the teller. "Oh, I saw her last week and someone pointed her out," I said, too quickly. I saw a glance pass from Ricky to Rachel. "I thought they broke up. I mean, isn't that what Brian had said about her at Caruso's, Rick?"

Ricky shrugged. "I don't remember his exact words," he said.

"It's getting cold," Rachel said. "Lax looks tired." She picked him up and rocked him in her arms while I held onto the limp leash. "Let's go home."

"You okay, Rachel?" Ricky asked so sympathetically I wanted to throw up. She nodded. We walked the rest of the way in silence.

"Thanks for walking Lax with me," Rachel said when we reached her house. She squeezed my hand, smiled at Ricky, and disappeared into her house with Lax and the leash that I surrendered unhappily.

"I'd be pretty worried if I were you," Ricky said

after she was gone. "I don't think it's a coincidence those guys and Beth were at your game."

"Probably not," I agreed. "Especially Beth."

"What's the scoop on her?" he asked, as we headed for his car.

"Nothing. She called one night to talk about Brian. She says she's scared of him but she still goes for him. She's as weird as her boyfriend. Pretty screwed-up chick, I guess."

"That's for sure," he said. "Seems all the good-looking ones are that way, doesn't it?"

I stared at him hard. "What's that supposed to mean?" I asked.

"Oh, don't go busting your chops," he said, unlocking the doors of his car. "You've got to admit your girlfriend can get confusing."

"It doesn't bother me," I said. "Does it bother you?" I swear I would have fought him on the spot if he said one more word about Rachel. I was dying to hear him say something nasty about her. I would have fought him till my hands broke off.

Instead, he shook his head and stared at me for a long minute. "No," he finally said. "Why should it bother me? Let's get out of here. I've got some homework to finish. Hop in already."

"No thanks," I said. "I'd rather walk."

"You're nuts," Ricky, the future shrink, declared, and without waiting to hear another word, I broke into a killer run and ran all the way home. I don't know why I ran so fast. Maybe I was scared. Of Brian and his buddies. Of Beth Levine. Of Rachel. Of Ricky. Of just about everybody I could think of.

•16

I had three messages from Beth Levine when I got home from Rachel's. "She sure was anxious to speak to you," my mother told me. "Oh, by the way, Pam called, too. The list keeps growing."

"Yeah, I can't keep track of all of them," I said. I heard the way her voice dropped when she mentioned Pam.

"Why does 'Beth Levine' sound so familiar?" she asked as I headed to my room.

"Beats me," I lied. Of course, I remembered that she'd heard about Brian Murphy's Jewish girlfriend from my father, but I wasn't about to remind her. I had enough problems for one night. I wanted to call Beth back as soon as possible.

"Well, hi there, Mr. Jock," Beth greeted me, as friendly as could be. "I've been waiting for your call all night. How've you been?"

"Fine," I said. "But I was surprised to hear you and your old boyfriend showed up at my lacrosse game today."

"Oh, don't be surprised by anything Brian Murphy does," she said. "If I had one piece of advice for you, that would be it."

"Well, if I had one piece of advice for you," I answered her, "it would be to stay away from public places with Brian Murphy until his trial is over."

"I'm not like that," she said. "I don't turn my back on my friends when they're in trouble."

"Yeah, I can see that," I said. "But I didn't think you wanted your parents to know about this loyalty to old friends." I wasn't usually so bold talking to girls, but there was something about this Beth Levine that made me feel different around her than I felt around other girls. As good-looking as she was, I didn't like her or anything like that. But I was sort of interested in what made her tick.

"I don't," she said, "but it's just a matter of time until they see that Brian is innocent and this whole stupid matter is solved. Which is why I called you. I want you to tell your father to concentrate on looking for the person who did write this graffiti and leave poor Brian alone."

"Oh, I see," I said. "Now, let me try and get this whole thing straight. Last time we talked, you told me it was his mother who did it. Is that who you want my dad's office to concentrate on?"

"No, but—"

"Look, Beth," I interrupted her, "I've got a lot of work to do tonight. And I really don't feel in the mood for this conversation. So, if you don't mind, I'd just as soon end it now."

"I'm not quite through, Zack." Beth's voice was all business now. "You seem like a nice kid. I like everything I learn about you. And, believe it or not, so does Brian. He even liked your girlfriend, Rachel Levy. We both liked watching her today. So, a nice kid like you ought to know that his father is making a big mistake. Believe me, Zack, Brian did not write that graffiti. So you tell that to your father. Oh, and that dog is so cute, Zack. And what a perfect name, Lax. Adorable."

"Are you threatening me, Beth?" I couldn't believe my ears. This girl was threatening the family and friends and pet of the friends of the family of the D.A.! Who could keep it all straight? It was bad enough that Tony had threatened Sam, but now Beth was doing the same thing. Sam, Rachel, Lax. Maybe I should just tie the three of them up into one big package and deliver it to Brian's front door. He and his mother could scribble graffiti all over the three of them in Brian's bedroom on the floor right underneath his lacrosse trophies and high honor roll awards.

"Threatening you?" Beth repeated indignantly. "What are you saying? I'm your friend. And I help my friends. Just the way I'm sure you take care of your friends. This is no threat. Don't be silly. We're both Jewish, aren't we? Jews don't threaten Jews. We stick together. Boy, Zack, you are strange. Listen, I've got to run. I promised I'd call Brian after I spoke to you. I'm sure you really weren't surprised to hear we're back together again. You can't separate people who truly care about each other. I'm sure that's what happened between you and your girlfriend, Rachel. Last time we talked, you two were history. Now look at you. You're probably as close as me and Brian. Now he wanted me to be sure that I gave you the important message. Look for someone else. Take care. And good luck protecting your net."

I was stunned. I wasn't crazy. That girl *had* threatened me and my girlfriend and my girlfriend's dog. I knew what I had to do. I was going to tell my father exactly what Beth had told me. I must have been nuts to have been interested in this girl. She was one dangerous chick.

My mother had no idea when my father would be home. "He ran back to the office as soon as you left for Rachel's," she told me. "He's working on the Murphy case. God, I'll be glad when this case is over. So, what did that nice Levine girl want?"

"How do you know she's nice?" I asked her.

"Because I remembered who she is," my mother answered. "I'm sure she's sorry she was ever mixed up with that hoodlum."

"But you're still sure she's nice?" I asked again.

"Well, I know she comes from a nice family."

"Oh, really? That's all it takes to be nice? To come from a nice family? You know, Mom, you're wrong. Actually, I think it's prejudiced of you to think like that. You think every girl who comes from a nice Jewish family is nice and every girl who comes from a non-Jewish family is not nice. And I don't think that's nice."

"My goodness, Zack, you certainly are touchy tonight," she said. "I didn't mean to say that all your friends should be Jewish. I just want you to try and date Jewish girls as often as you can. It means a lot to your grandparents and to Dad and me that you marry a Jewish girl."

"I can't stand it!" I yelled. "I'm fifteen years old and you're worried about who I'm going to marry! I could think of a lot more serious things for you to worry about. Like if I'm alive in ten years."

"My God, you're dramatic tonight," my mom said. She looked at me real funny, like she couldn't decide if I was being serious or not. When the phone rang, she was still looking at me. She had begun to get some of that old panicky look in her eyes, and I was regretting every nasty word I'd just said to her. I had no one to blame but myself if she started driving me to school again. Thank God, it was my aunt Toby. That conversation would be good for an hour.

I made up my mind right then and there. Enough pussyfooting around. Enough being messed up by Beth and messing up Rachel's mind. There were answers out there and I was going to find them. My father's office was lost on this case. They were working night and day and couldn't figure out if Brian had done this thing by himself. It was time for someone else to figure out what was going on, someone with fresh new ideas. I thought about calling Ricky and working out some kind of a plan with him, but that thought lasted about a second. This was one plan I was going to have to concoct and execute myself.

I grabbed my jacket and slid out the front door, closing the door very quietly behind me. It was funny, but I had never left my house before without telling my parents where I was going. Oh, I might have lied about my whereabouts, saying I was going to Ricky's house when I was really going to Pam's, or saying that I was going to the library when I was going to hang out with my friends, but that was about it. But this night was different. I knew where I was going: Brian Murphy's house.

It took me about a half hour and two buses to get to Rockville, but at ten past ten that night, I was standing outside the Murphy house. I was surprised that it was such a small house. I don't know what I was expecting, but I had assumed the house would be the same size as mine. Mr. Murphy was a dentist, after all. But his house was about half the size of ours. It was dark on the first floor, but all the rooms on the second floor were well lit. The truth was I had no real plan. All I had planned was to get to the house. I figured that the rest of my plan would come to me once I got there. It didn't.

I was standing on the sidewalk in front of the house when I noticed the front door open. Without thinking, I raced over to the big tree to the right of the house and crouched down behind it. From my position, I saw a large man wearing a black leather jacket walk down the front stairs and head toward the driveway. Although it was dark, I could see the man's face as he passed by the streetlight on the way to the driveway. He had a lot of black hair and a mustache. He looked a little bit like Brian, but he was taller and heavier. I knew right away that he had to be Brian's dad. I didn't give myself a chance to think. Instead, I just popped out from behind the tree and walked over to the man. He moved back quickly, nearly crashing into his car.

"Excuse me," I said, louder than I intended. "Are you Mr. Murphy?"

"Who the hell are you?" he asked me, straightening himself up.

I should have been frightened or at least concerned about what I was getting myself into, but I wasn't. All I cared about was getting some answers to some questions that were making a mess out of my life. "I'm Zack Stone," I told him. "Are you Brian's father?"

"Oh, brother," he said, leaning against his car and taking a good look at me. "The D.A.'s son. If I'm not mistaken, this feels like harassment from the D.A.'s office."

"It's not," I said. "So you are Mr. Murphy."

"Yes, I am Dr. Murphy," he said, mimicking my tone. "Did you come here to talk to me or to ask my son to come out and play lacrosse?"

I remembered how my father had said that Dr. Murphy seemed like a nice man. There didn't seem to be anything nice about him now. Of course, maybe he just didn't like strangers appearing in his driveway, uninvited, late at night. "I came to talk to you," I answered him. "I'd actually like to talk to you and Brian together, if that is possible."

"Oh, you would, would you?" he said. "Well, I'm afraid that would be impossible. My son's not up to talking to you right now. He's doing his homework. You understand about homework, don't you? My son's an excellent student. I'm sure you get very good grades in school, too, don't you?"

"I'm a good student," I said. "Could I speak to you for a few minutes?"

"No, I'm afraid that wouldn't be possible either," he said. "You see, all us Murphys are kind of busy now and the last person we'd like to talk to is a Stone. Now I think you better get off my property before I have to call the police and ask them to get you out of here. That might be a little embarrassing for your father, don't you think? This is your father's case, isn't it? Has he hired you to work for his office on this case?"

I couldn't figure this man out. There was something sort of nice about him. The way he was smiling at me and looking me over. And his tone was kind of light, almost like he was joking with me. But there was also something nasty about him. It was his eyes, I decided. He had weird, kind of shifty eyes. He was looking at me, but he really wasn't. And that mustache. I hated that mustache. He reminded me of a lacrosse coach I'd had for a year in the seventh grade. He'd had a mustache, too. I had never been able to figure out that guy either. I could never tell if he was smiling or smirking at me. That was how I felt about Dr. Murphy. "I don't work for my father," I answered him. "He'd have a bird if he knew I was here."

"You're disobeying your father?" he said, shaking his head back and forth in this fake surprise. He was making fun of me. That much, I could figure out. "How shocking. A nice boy like you, disobeying his father. Well, I think you better leave now before you disobey him any further."

"Did Brian write that graffiti by himself?" I asked. "I need to know."

"You don't need to know anything," he told me, "but I'll tell you something, anyhow. Brian did not write that graffiti by himself, okay? Does that answer your question, Mr. Stone? Now will you go home?"

He was enjoying this. He was having a good time with me. I was making an idiot of myself, and he was loving every second of watching me do that. For some reason, I didn't mind making a fool of myself. It was okay. So I continued. "If he didn't do it by himself, who did he do it with?"

"Boy, you don't give up, do you?" Dr. Murphy smiled. "And you do ask tough questions, just like your old man. You'll probably grow up to be a district attorney just like him." He leaned back against the car and stared at me. "I just might give you that answer," he finally said, his face covered with that smile-smirk. "But first you need to answer a few questions for me. Okay?"

I nodded.

"First, tell me why you want to know. What's it to you, anyhow? You're not the D.A. What's it matter to you if my son did it alone or with a posse?"

"Because I am involved," I said. "I'm Jewish and I saw the graffiti and it sickened me. It also sickens my girlfriend. Her parents are survivors. They were at one of the concentration camps written on the temple."

"Yeah, well, that's a different story." Dr. Murphy's face darkened. Now, there was no smile. He was no longer humoring me. He was getting angry. "And it's one I could care less about. Enough with you and your questions. You're on my property, in case you didn't notice. Now get lost. I'm busy."

"I know you are," I said. "But you said you had a few questions to ask me. You only asked me one. What else did you want to ask me?"

He stared hard and long at me. "It has to do with

your father,'' he said. "I want you to tell me if he's a good father. Tell me the truth. Not what you think you should say. Is the D.A. a good father?''

"He is,'' I said.

"Yeah? Why?'' he asked.

" 'Cause he's always there,'' I said. "He cares about me.''

"That's all it takes to be a good father?'' he asked. "Caring and being there?''

"I think so. Plus, I respect him.''

"Oh, you do, do you? Isn't that nice? Now, one last question. Are you a good son?''

"I don't know,'' I said. "I'm probably not being a good son now, coming here and talking to you like this, but most times, I think I am.''

"Tell me how you manage that, Mr. Stone.''

"I try and listen to him, and, like I said, I respect him. If he wants me to do something, I do it.''

"Aha,'' Mr. Murphy grinned. "That's it, isn't it? You do what he wants. That's the key, Zack, my boy. You do what your father wants. Now, if you'll excuse me, I have to get going. I need to meet a friend.''

Before I could say another word, he had climbed into the driver's seat of his car and slammed the door in my face. He hadn't answered my question at all, I thought miserably as I watched him drive his car out of his driveway.

I walked halfway home and took the bus the rest of the way. I didn't get home till midnight. My house looked huge as I studied it from the sidewalk. I was standing there for the longest time, when it hit me. Dr. Murphy had answered my question. That strange, half-nice, half-scary man had given me the answer to my question. Brian had not done the graffiti by himself. And his father had told me who he had done it with.

17

My father was sitting by himself at the kitchen table, reading his mail and eating frozen yogurt, when I walked into the house. He was so startled when he saw me that he dropped his spoon on the floor. "Your mother said you'd gone to bed," he said. "Where the hell were you?"

"I went to Brian Murphy's house," I told him. I was so relieved my mother wasn't there with him.

"Brian Murphy's house?" My father was getting all red in the face. I was afraid he was going to wake my mother.

"I know what you're thinking," I said quickly, trying to head him off at the pass before he called in the recruits, namely, my mother. "I shouldn't have done that. But you weren't home and I just had to do something. Beth Levine called me tonight. She sort of threatened me. She said if I didn't find out who did the graffiti and stop blaming Brian, something might happen to me. Or Rachel."

My father was no longer red. Now he was white. I'd never seen him look like that. It was making me very nervous. I was almost wishing the recruits would come into the room. But I continued talking.

"I don't know—maybe I was imagining the threats. But I couldn't just sit here and do nothing, so I went to Brian's house."

"What exactly were you planning to do at Brian's house?" my father asked when I paused to catch my breath. "Interrogate him? Search his room? Handcuff him and bring him down to headquarters? Whatever was going through your mind, Zack?"

"I don't know, Dad. I was sick of sitting around watching Rachel go nutty and having Beth Levine threaten me. I wanted to talk to Brian, man to man."

"Unbelievable. I can't believe you, of all people, could act so irrationally and so irresponsibly." My father wasn't shouting at me the way he usually did when he got angry. He looked sick. I couldn't remember ever feeling worse about anything I'd done to upset him.

"I didn't see him, Dad," I said, sitting in the kitchen chair next to him.

"Well, thank God for minor miracles," my father said, and I noticed a little bit of color was coming back into his cheeks. "Because it could have been catastrophic for the whole case—never mind your personal safety—if you'd actually made contact with him."

"I saw his father," I said softly.

"His father!" My father's scream should have brought my mother downstairs in a flash. "You saw Ray Murphy!"

"Yeah," I said. "I talked to him for a few minutes. Outside his house. He was sort of nice. He told me who did the graffiti with Brian." My father's mouth was wide open. I could see the fillings in his back teeth. "He did it, Dad. He and Brian did it together or Dr. Murphy made him do it. I'm not sure exactly what happened, but Brian was obeying his father's orders."

My father closed his mouth and stared at me. "I don't know what to say," he finally said. "I'm beyond furious over what you did. It was dead wrong. But I have this crazy feeling you busted open this miserable case. Keep your jacket on. I'll grab mine and call Patty. We're going down to my office right now."

Things happened very quickly from then on. My father drove me to his office where Patty was waiting for us. I repeated every word of my conversation with Dr. Murphy into the microphone of a tape recorder. Then my father drove me home. I was so exhausted by then, I couldn't think straight. I did, however, think about calling Rachel, but I guess some part of my brain was still operating, and I collapsed on my bed and fell asleep, my head aching, without touching the phone.

School the next day was a blur for me, but by the time my father came home from work very late that night, he understood everything. After a series of phone calls from my father's office to Brian's lawyer, Dr. Murphy and Mr. Donahue had come into my father's office that evening and filled in all the missing details. Dr. Murphy, the well-respected dentist, was an anti-Semite. He also hated African Americans, Latinos, and Asians, but he had a special aversion for Jews. Yet, when he'd found out that Brian was dating a Jewish girl, he had tried to swallow his rage. He had let Brian know he wasn't psyched over his girlfriend, but he did an okay job of staying out of his son's social life.

"He knew his son would have lots of girlfriends," my father explained to my mother the next morning as I tried to swallow my breakfast. "He figured this romance would last a few weeks and then blow over. But when he found out the Levines had made their daughter break up with his son, he went crazy. All his thinly covered rage came out of the closet." The big thing, to both my parents, was that Dr. Murphy had such power over his son. Somehow, he forced Brian to write the graffiti. It was a lesson for Brian. To teach him that thousands of other people had hated Jews. And that they had good reason to.

"It's hard for me to believe that this intelligent, law-abiding man didn't realize his son might have to go to jail because of that," my father continued as I stuffed my books into my backpack. "I guess, at the time of the incident, he lost touch with reality. Murphy claims he was ready to confess before he spoke to Zack that night. He kept hoping it would all blow over. I can't understand why it took him this long to realize it wouldn't. My God, we indicted his kid." Just to be sure, they made Dr. Murphy take a lie detector test. He passed it. He was coming in today for some psychiatric tests now, but my father was willing to bet everything that now he was finally telling the truth.

"Something was strange about this case from the beginning," my dad repeated for what had to be the hundredth time. "Thanks to Zack, we're beginning to find out what." There was still a lot of confusion about the case, but Brian was in less deep than he'd been at his indictment. He was still guilty of writing the graffiti on the temple, but the case had a new slant. You had to feel sorry for the kid for having a crazy father. My father agreed with that. He felt sorry for Brian, but he was certain that in the end, after a lot of hard work, justice would be served. Clint Eastwood was back in the saddle.

More than anything, I was shocked that my mother didn't snap over what I'd done. I had begged my dad not to tell her, but he was adamant about there being no secrets in our house. My mother had gasped and carried on for about an hour, but then she'd calmed down. "You acted impetuously and stupidly," she told me, in case I didn't already know. "But I can *almost* understand why. This time you were lucky. You didn't get your head blown off. I hope to God you'll never do such a stupid thing again. I've got to tell you, Zack, I can worry about you just so much. I'll die an early death if I worry any more than I already do. I can't believe this whole mess is finally being put to rest."

"Thanks, in large part, to the stupidity of our older son," my father said when she was through.

I left for school with the same headache I'd gone to bed with for the past two nights. There was too much to digest and I was worn out trying to swallow everything my father had handed us. I knew I had only myself to blame for my family's overinvolvement with this case, but I was beginning to wish I'd never heard of Brian Murphy. So I'd helped settle the whole mess. Big deal. Dr. Murphy was going to confess, anyhow. My life still felt out of control. Why, I asked myself as I grabbed my jacket, couldn't my father have been a plumber? Luckily, my father had told me, no one at school would know what had happened the night before, and I was determined to try and put it out of my mind. For one school day, anyhow. I mean, it was all unbelievable, but I did have a life of my own. And Brian and Dr. Murphy weren't the most important people in it.

Ricky appeared at my house ten minutes early. "We have to talk now," he announced as soon as I got into his car. I didn't want to talk to Ricky about anything more personal than what I'd eaten for breakfast, but I had no choice. "I think we better clear the air about Rachel once and for all."

That was so typical of Ricky. Nothing could just slip by. It was a miracle he'd let two nights go by before hitting me with this "clear the air" stuff. It was like he'd already gone to medical school and become a psychiatrist. And I was his lucky first patient. "Look, I'm sorry for the way I acted the other night," I said. "I just got bent out of shape about you and Rachel. Now that she and I are back together, I'm getting over my jealousy. Give me a little time.''

"I'll give you all the time you want,'' he said. "I understand why you were jealous. Rachel and I got close last week. She's something else. The more I got to know her, the more I could see that.''

I wasn't enjoying this conversation. "That's true,'' I said. "I'm lucky to have gotten her back. I'll be more careful with her now.''

"Well, that's what I wanted to talk to you about.''

I was enjoying it less and less by the second. "Yeah? Why?''

"This isn't easy for me, man.'' Ricky didn't seem all that happy with the conversation either. Too bad he couldn't have just shut up. "But I need to tell you this. I like the girl. A lot.''

"I could tell that.''

"You could? I didn't realize that.''

"Yeah, well, I could. Anybody could. But it makes it kind of a mess.''

"Look, just tell me to get out of her life, and I will,'' Ricky said. "I just need you to tell me that, and I'll get out.''

"Well, exactly how much are you in it?''

"She's nuts over you, Zack. You know that. But we were working on kind of a special rapport last week. She tells me a lot of personal things.''

"Oh, you're sort of like her shrink, huh?''

"I guess you might put it like that. But I'm not expressing myself very well. You're my best friend. You've been my best friend for as far back as I can remember. I don't want some girl to interfere with that. But I'm in a bind 'cause I can't get her out of my mind. I have to be honest with you. If you want me to back off, just tell me and consider it done.''

"Back off.''

"Sure."

That was the end of our conversation. It was kind of quiet as we drove the last few minutes to school. But I didn't have one more word to say to him, and it was pretty obvious he didn't have anything to say to me. We walked silently toward our lockers. "See you later," he said when he reached his. I nodded without looking at him and walked on to mine.

Rachel was standing by my locker, looking awesome. Everything crazy in my life seemed to fade away when I saw her, smiling and waiting for me. "Hi, handsome," she greeted me and kissed my cheek. "Can you come out with me and my parents for dinner tonight?" she asked. "It's my mother's birthday. She asked me to invite you."

"Hey, I'd be honored," I told her.

Rachel beamed. "She'll be thrilled. I'll call her right now, so she can make a reservation somewhere. See you at lunch."

The rest of the day was wonderfully uneventful. I could tell Ricky was nervous around me, but there was nothing I could do about that. I knew the two of us had to talk about Rachel again, but it would have to wait a bit. I felt bad for Ricky. He liked Rachel a lot. But she was my girl. He'd have to accept that. And I'd have to work on my jealousy. At least, I knew I wasn't totally crazy. I'd been right to feel jealous. He'd been making a play for Rachel. When I thought about it, it kind of scared me. If you can't trust your best friend, who could you trust?

Dinner with the Levys was great. Mrs. Levy looked real happy when I got to their house. Mr. Levy wore a suit and tie and shook my hand warmly. Luckily, my mom had insisted I wear a jacket and tie when I told her we were going to Jimmy's Harborside. Actually, I was wearing a blue blazer, the only jacket I had that fit me, new chinos that my mother picked up on her way home from the shelter, and a light blue button-down shirt with a red and white tie with lacrosse sticks on it. Sam'd given me the tie for my birthday and I like it. It makes me feel like a jock when I wear it.

"Wow, do you look handsome," Rachel said when she saw me. Of course, she looked beautiful. We might have been through some hard times, but that was behind us. The Brian Murphy mystery was over. Everything was turning out just the way I had hoped.

The four of us drove to Jimmy's Harborside in Mr. Levy's Camry. It felt weird to be sitting in the backseat with Mr. and Mrs. Levy in front, sort of like one big happy family. Things were so confusing in my own house, with my father still stressed out by the Murphy case and my mother going nuts trying to find housing for a litter of ten German shepherd puppies, that it was a relief to be with this family. Every now and then I would remember what Rachel had told me about her parents' experiences in the concentration camps, but that night, it was hard to imagine such nightmarish scenes in this family's past.

Mrs. Levy was sixty-two. That seemed so old but she didn't look that old to me. Mr. Levy made a nice toast to her before the meal. "To the most wonderful wife and mother in the universe," he said as he held up his wineglass. He had poured a little white wine for me and Rachel. "A woman as beautiful inside as she is on the outside. How lucky can one man be?"

Mrs. Levy cried a little during the toast and kissed her husband after he sipped his wine. I was embarrassed by the whole scene, and so was Rachel. She shrugged her shoulders and I grinned back at her.

"So, what great pieces of literature are you reading these days?" Mr. Levy asked me when our main courses were served. Jimmy's is a real popular fish restaurant, but I ordered chicken piccata since I'm not all that nuts over fish. Both Mr. and Mrs. Levy had some kind of fancy salmon in paper bag, and Rachel had broiled scrod. I made sure that my dish didn't cost any more than Rachel's.

"Oh, we're doing poetry this week," I told him. "Robert Browning's 'My Last Duchess.' Man, was that Duke one crazy guy."

Mr. Levy laughed. "I love Browning. His narrative poems are fun. His characters are all crazy, but you can't help being fascinated by them."

"We read another one about some guy who strangles his girlfriend because he's jealous of her," I said.

" 'Porphyria's Lover,' " he said. "Wonderful symbolism in that poem."

"I like 'Rabbi Ben Ezra,' " Rachel said. "But, most of all, I love his wife's *Sonnets from the Portuguese.* They make me cry."

"They are beautiful," Mr. Levy agreed. "But now they're saying that their marriage was not as beautiful as the sonnets."

"Oh, I can't stand the way all the biographers have to search until they find some unpleasant facts," Mrs. Levy said. "But I guess no one wants to buy some biography that says the famous person was an ordinary man."

"Who's your favorite writer?" I asked Mrs. Levy.

"Oh, I don't know," she said.

"You cried over *The Bridges of Madison County,*" Rachel said. "I never saw you cry so much over a book."

"I know," Mrs. Levy admitted. "I don't know what got into me. It was such a silly book, but it touched me. But Elie Weisel's books touch me, too."

There was an awkward silence at our table after she

mentioned Weisel. I remembered that Rachel had said Weisel was one of the reasons her father had come to B.U. I wondered if the Levys had met him in a concentration camp. That thought sent shivers up my spine. I really had to read one of his books on the Holocaust. "I've never read any of his books," I admitted, breaking the silence. "I'm going to, though."

"I know Rachel told you about our histories," Mr. Levy said. "How Ruth and I are survivors of the Holocaust. I'm afraid it makes us a bit different than other American Jews. It even makes Rachel different than other American Jews. We have a history. A terrible one. But I don't want to spoil Ruth's special night. Tonight is a night of celebration and pleasure. It's not every day that my wife turns sixty-two."

"I can't believe you're sixty-two, Mama," Rachel said. She'd turned kind of pale during her father's discussion, but her color was coming back now. "That seems so old. It's funny. Diane's mom is only thirty-four, but in many ways you seem younger than her."

"That's because Naomi Halpert's had three husbands," Mr. Levy said. "That will age you faster than anything else in this world."

The rest of the evening was fun and relaxed. Maybe it's because Rachel is an only child, but she has a different relationship with her parents than I do with mine. The Levys seem like three friends. Maybe, it's because Rachel's a girl. The Levys are also more sophisticated than my family. In my house; there's always some sort of a catastrophe. A sick or homeless animal, an ugly court case, a visiting relative, a broken stove or refrigerator—just something that gets everybody all upset and excited. That's the word: excited. The Stones are always excited. Oh, sure, some of the excitement comes from me, my problems over a lacrosse game or with an exam or a teacher. But that's just our family's style: excitable.

The Levys are different. They're calmer and real charming. I liked talking about literature with Mr. Levy. I couldn't imagine doing that with my dad. He's interested in all my schoolwork and my lacrosse games, but we'd never discuss a poem. Plus, he would never sit still long enough to have such a discussion. He'd have to get up to answer a phone call or check something in the oven or pour himself a glass of juice or clean up a spot on the floor, just as we were getting into the discussion. I'm not saying that's bad. That's just the way he is.

After we left the restaurant, the Levys drove me home. "Thank you both for such a terrific evening," I said as I got out of the car.

"Our pleasure," Mr. Levy said. "It made my wife's birthday celebration very special to have you with us."

Rachel gave me a quick kiss on my cheek before I left the car. She looked as happy as I felt. As I walked into my house, I had the weirdest feeling that everything in my life was just too good to be true. For once, I couldn't have been more correct.

•18

I'm not sure how it all happened, but our lacrosse team made it to the state finals. As mediocre as we'd been at the beginning of the season, we just kept getting stronger, knocking off all the other top contenders. It was the first time in the history of our high school that the lacrosse team had made it so far. Coach Wetherbee insisted that it was due to me, that when I was hot there was no player who could cool me off, but I discounted his theory. The truth was our first line, including Dana, Paul Edelman and Keldog Kelly, was unstoppable. Those guys scored, no matter who was guarding the opposing cage. I know I'm important, but all I can do is keep balls out of the net. Someone has to score, and those three forwards were the guys.

Everyone in school was psyched about the upcoming tournament. Girls I barely knew stopped me in the corridor to tell me how great I was playing. Teachers—including my crotchety old math teacher Miss London, who wouldn't recognize a lacrosse stick if she tripped over one—went out of their way to tell me how proud they were of my lacrosse accomplishments.

Rachel was even more excited than my mom. She got her soccer team to put up dozens of posters about the tournament all over the school. Some of them even had newspaper pictures of me in the net. The girl was incredible.

Ricky was still trying to get our friendship back on track, but I just couldn't seem to feel normal around him. I knew he still liked Rachel, and it made me uneasy every time he mentioned her name. I spoke to him briefly when he called me on the phone and answered him when he said something to me in school, but I no longer dialed his number or accepted rides in his car. I turned sixteen two days before the championship game, anyhow, so it was just six months until I had my own license. Until then, Keldog was willing to pick me up in the morning.

The weekend before the game, Coach Wetherbee had us practicing both Saturday and Sunday until it got dark. Sunday evening, I was so exhausted after our practice that I could barely eat dinner. My mother had made a vegetable lasagna that I liked and my father had baked my favorite pecan pie. I wanted to eat a lot and be pleasant during our meal, but it was too much of an effort. The excitement of the games was beginning to get to me, and I knew that the sooner I got into my room and put on my stereo, the better off I would be. But my parents didn't have a clue as to how I was feeling.

"I'm taking the afternoon off tomorrow," my father told me. "I want to get to Worcester early so I can get a good position for my video camera. I thought I might interview the team on video before the game. If it's okay with you."

"Please, Dad," I begged, "don't do that. It'll make me more nervous."

My father held up his hands. "Okay. No pregame interviews. Bad idea. I'll be so inconspicuous you'll have no idea I'm there. I promise."

"Oh, sure," I moaned. "You and your video camera are as inconspicuous as Mom and her fifty greyhounds."

"I'm not bringing a dog to the game," my mother said.

"Right!" I said. "And the moon is made of cheese."

"I'm serious," she insisted, "and I'm wearing a black jacket and jeans."

Now I was getting worried. "You mean, you won't be decked out in Bromley's colors? You won't be wearing your red and black coat, red hat with the black pompom, and red sneakers with the black laces? Come on. What's happening here? Are the Stones turning normal?"

"We just want you to enjoy this exciting moment in your life," my mom said, sounding like a greeting card.

"Yeah, well, I'll try," I said. "But to tell you the truth, I'm kind of tired. I need to get some homework done and a good night's sleep."

"I'll throw the ball around with you in the basement for a few minutes, if you want," Sam offered.

"Great," I said, standing up and pushing back my chair. The kid always had a way of helping my game. I'd given up trying to figure out how he did it, but he'd watch me throw and make a suggestion that improved my arm.

"No dessert for either of you?" my father asked, looking as if we'd both slugged him in the stomach.

"Later, Dad," Sam said, and I followed my little brother out of the kitchen.

I tried to get to bed early that night, but there was no way sleep was going to come easily. Since I was a little kid, I'd always had a problem falling asleep on Sunday evenings. It was after eleven and I was lying on my bed, staring at my unbelievable poster of a man staring at the Vietnam Wall when the phone rang. I grabbed it on the first ring. It was Beth Levine. "I just wanted to warn you," she said in an icy tone. "You're in for a tough time tomorrow."

Something about her voice made me angry. "Well, how nice of you to warn me," I said, my own voice dripping with sarcasm. "But then again what are nice Jewish friends for?"

"I'm not your friend, Zack. But someone else hates you a lot more than I do. And he's playing on Worcester's lacrosse team." The click after she hung up the phone sounded like the metallic slamming of a jail cell door. Old Beth probably held the key to that cell, but I knew she'd swallow it before letting me get my hands on it.

Without thinking, I dialed Ricky's phone number. When I heard his sleepy, "Hello," I knew I'd woken him. And I also knew I had no right to call him. Some wires in my brain had been momentarily crossed and I'd forgotten that we were no longer best friends. I hung up the phone without saying a word. I did fall asleep that night—in a sleeping bag on the floor of Sam's room.

•19

I was so lousy during our warm-up practice in Worcester before the championship game that Coach Wetherbee was ready to bring in Chip Norris. It was only when Dana went down on his hands and knees and pleaded with him to put me in for the game that the coach gave me the go-ahead. It wasn't that the kids from Worcester were so huge, which they were, that was getting to me. I'd played against bigger teams. In lacrosse, it doesn't necessarily matter how big you are, it's speed. You can be a monster, but if your legs can't move, you're not going to get that ball in the net. But knowing that one of those big thugs was aiming for my head, not so he could score a goal but so he could end my life, had an effect on my head as well as my legs.

"Miserable jerk," I muttered to myself when the referee blew the whistle to begin the game. "You knew what you were doing when you called me last night. You were psyching me out. Well, better luck next time, Beth. 'Cause I'm in this game not just to survive but to win." The Worcester forward scored on me in the first eleven seconds of the game.

But, from then on, I was okay. It was as if I'd had to give up that one goal in order to get rid of the dust on my brain. During the first period, I had three saves that surprised even me. Somehow or other, the net on my stick got to where the ball was heading before the ball got there. It was eerie. The crowd was humongous. And even though the game was being held in Worcester, Bromley had as big a cheering section as the home team. When all the action was down at the Worcester net, I did a few minutes of serious crowd searching and immediately found my parents and Rachel. My mom and Rachel had their arms around each other. I saw my father's video camera trained on me even though both teams were down at the other end of the field. I waved my stick at him. And then flung myself back into the game as the horde of Worcester giants came racing over to trample me.

By the end of the third period, the score was tied three all. I'd made twenty-two saves, and the two Worcester goalies had racked up six each. There was no doubt our opponents were stronger than us, but I'd never seen my teammates work so hard. I always want to win, but at the beginning of the fourth and final period, I wanted to win so badly every nerve in my body was on fire. I could practically taste the victory. I felt as if I'd been through such a tough time, what with all the problems with Brian and Rachel, that I just had to have this win for my team. Beth's words of warning still rang in my ears, but I was determined to use them as an impetus, rather than as a deterrent. It would serve her right if we won.

The last period turned out to be a killer. Worcester grew stronger while we were struggling to keep our heads above water. At one point, the balls were leaping at me so furiously, I made five saves in four minutes. And then it happened. I saw the attackman cradling the ball as he hurdled toward me. He was the same guy who had scored twice on me already. He was big. Very big. I was banging my stick against the outside of the cage, trying to focus on the ball that was making its way too quickly toward my net, when this amazon passed the ball to a teammate and charged me. "Kike!" he screamed into my face as he knocked me down. "Death to the miserable kikes!"

Before I went down, I saw the guy's eyes. Even through his helmet, I could see his eyes—eyes filled with a hatred that made Tony Caruso's eyes look like those of a greyhound. I fell down and the ball sailed over my head into the net. I waited for the referee to blow his whistle, but the sound never came. It's one thing for an attackman to bang into a goalie when he's charging the net and the goalie's in his way. But it's another thing when the goalie's out of the play and an attackman nails him. That's a deliberate hit away from the ball that calls for a five-minute penalty. Something was wrong here. The lower part of my back stung like crazy when I hit the ground. But there was no way I was going to be put out of this game. Not by one powerful but illegal hit, anyhow. As Dana and Paul helped me up, Dana said, "What the heck's going on here? That cheap tank ran you over for no reason. And nobody called a penalty."

I saw stars as I stood up, but when Coach Wetherbee started to race over to me, I waved him off. There were two and a half minutes left in this game and no way was I going out. Not unless it was on a stretcher, which, even in my delirium, I understood was a possibility. I knew I had a choice. Either I concentrate on the anti-Semite who was determined to kill me or I think about the rest of his team and protect the cage and not my ass. I chose the cage.

As a reward, Dana and "Keldog" doubled up on my assassin. The 150 seconds seemed like an eternity, but when the final whistle was blown, Worcester was on top by one. It hurt so much I wanted to cry, but, of course, I didn't. Instead, I followed my teammates to the center of the field where we shook hands with the winners. I could have left the line before the monster and I met, but no way was I going to be a wimp. He grabbed my hand, squeezed it till the tears sprang to my eyes, and muttered, "Kikes never win."

And that did it. I pulled my hand free and shoved my face into his. "Oh, yeah!" I screamed into his eyes and nose and mouth. But it wasn't his face I was seeing. It was Rachel's. Beautiful brave Rachel telling me that her parents were survivors and how that had affected her life. God only knew what those two people had survived. This miserable animal was nothing in comparison to the fiends they must have faced. "Let me tell you that it's bigots like you who don't win! 'Cause you spend your whole pathetic lives hating and eventually that hate eats you up. Like poisonous worms. And you've got a bad case of the worms, buddy. It sure is going to be fun watching them eat you up."

Before the tub of lard could say a word, Wetherbee was beside me, smiling like a crazed politician, pulling me back into the line and staying with me until I'd shaken the hand of every guy on the team. I expected everyone to be staring at me, but there was so much noise in the background from the hysterical Worcester fans that hardly anyone, except the anti-Semitic blimp and Wetherbee, had probably heard me. "You were terrific, Zack," Wetherbee told me as we headed toward the bus. "You played the game of your life."

"He hit me late, Coach," I said, trying to ignore the pain in my lower back. It seemed to be spreading like wildfire up my back and down into my legs. "How come no one called a penalty?"

"I saw what happened, Zack," he told me as soon as he got me off the field. "You had to be blind to miss it. Don't worry. We're going to challenge the game. It was an illegal block. Something was wrong with the referee. But we've got it on film. Just relax, man. We'll take care of it. You were the greatest.''

I wanted to hug him, but instead, I turned around to see what the amazon was doing. He was standing in the same position in which I'd left him, staring at me. The rest of his teammates were jumping around the field, hugging one another and celebrating like crazy, but he was standing there, staring at me, all by himself. More than anything, I wanted to go over to him and ask him one simple question: ''Why do you hate me and all Jews so much?'' But I knew better. He couldn't answer that question any better than Brian Murphy's dad could. Dr. Murphy and Tony Caruso and Hitler and this attackman were all cut from the same cloth, and they hated me with a passion that could cripple me for the rest of my life. If I let it. I had no idea what was going to happen with this game. But whether we won or lost really didn't matter. I had to fight much tougher foes than those who played on the Worcester lacrosse team, foes I'd never known existed until this past month.

My father had a perfect shot of the intentional hit. Coach Wetherbee submitted my dad's video and the official game video to a special committee who investigated the incident and decided it was too confusing a situation to change the outcome of the game. So we lost.

''It's a bummer,'' my father said when he hung up after talking to Coach Wetherbee a week after the game.

''Maybe you should have the ADL investigate it,'' my mother suggested.

''Please don't do that,'' I said. ''Just let it be. We lost.'' I was feeling lousy that night. My back was aching. The orthopedic surgeon my mother had dragged me to said it was a light strain and as long as I stayed away from strenuous sports for two months, it would be okay. But some days, it hurt no matter how I sat or stood or lay down. "I'd just like to let the whole matter die."

"Well, I feel good knowing the Murphys will get what's coming to them," my mother said. There had been a lot of plea-bargaining and legal maneuverings. Brian was going to receive a one-year sentence, all of which would be suspended. He would be required to attend a four-month course on the Holocaust at Milford State College, volunteer in the athletic department of the Rockville Jewish Community Center, and go for counseling. He was also going to have to address the congregation of Temple Israel at a special Sabbath service. His father would receive a three-year sentence, which would also be suspended, and he, too, had to attend a Holocaust course and address the congregation. To me, it sounded as if they had come off scot-free, and no matter how much my father disagreed, explaining they both now had permanent records and had been convicted of misdemeanors and that Dr. Murphy would have a lot of problems with his dental practice because of the bad publicity, it didn't seem like much of a punishment. After all, they weren't going to see the inside of a jail cell.

I walked out of the kitchen and into Sam's room. He was lying on his floor, studying the constellations he'd drawn and put up on his ceiling. He'd covered his whole ceiling with black paper and drawn stars and planets all over the paper. It was remarkable. I lay down beside him. "What's that?" I asked, pointing to a particularly large and bright star.

"Venus," he answered. "It's a planet that moves at an orbit between Earth and Mercury. It's about sixty-seven million miles from the sun over there. It goes through phases similar to the moon. Sometimes, it's the brightest object in the sky. Amazing, huh?''

"Yeah,'' I agreed. "It sure is. I wouldn't mind taking a trip there and staying for a few millenniums.''

"You'd be bored crazy there,'' he said. "It's a lot more exciting on this planet. Believe me.''

"Okay,'' I said.

"You must be bummed about losing that game, huh?'' he asked.

"It doesn't make any sense,'' I said. "It's like there's this conspiracy against me. You know—the gorilla, the referee, even Wetherbee. They all seem to have decided I needed to be shoved around and taught a lesson.''

"You're feeling paranoid, I guess.''

"I am,'' I admitted. "Like the whole world is out to get me. Or at least to get the Jew who caused a big fuss about a little hate crime.''

"It's not easy being Jewish,'' Sam said.

"My sentiments exactly, buddy,'' I said. Sometimes it's scary how smart my little brother is.

"But we don't have much choice, do we?'' he asked.

"None that I can see,'' I agreed, and then I lay back on the floor, amazed that there was no pain in my back, and stared at those incredible stars until I fell asleep.

•20

Two weeks later, there was a big rally at Temple Israel. It wasn't my dad's idea, even though he was featured as one of the main speakers. The idea came from three ministers in Rockville who were upset about the defacing of the temple in their city. They made an announcement about it over the loudspeaker in our high school. I was embarrassed about it, especially when a lot of kids in my homeroom stared at me during the announcement. I guess everyone knew I'd been pretty wrapped up in the whole graffiti scene.

Just before he left for the rally, my father came up to my room to talk to me. He'd been real quiet at dinner, and I knew he was thinking about his upcoming speech. He looked tired, and I was beginning to wonder if he'd ever look cheerful and well rested again. A double murder case would be a piece of cake after this one.

"I know it hasn't been an easy time for you, Zack," he said, while I sat at my desk, trying to finish my math homework. Man, did those words make me feel guilty. I just had schoolwork and lacrosse and Rachel and Ricky to worry about. He looked like he had the weight of the entire world on his shoulders. "I've always tried hard not to bring my family into my professional life, to shield you from what happens in my office, but this time I wasn't able to do that. I can't even promise you that what happened at Temple Israel and to you won't happen again. About the only thing I can do is to make sure that Ray and Brian Murphy pay for their crimes. The three of us spent a lot of time in court this past week, and I understand a lot more about this case than I did before."

"Yeah? Like the father and son duo is also into heavy drugs and interstate firearms smuggling?" I didn't mean to sound sarcastic, but the mere mention of Brian Murphy rankled my nerves. I knew that he hadn't been personally responsible for all my problems, but there was no denying my life had been a lot easier before he'd entered it.

"I don't know about that," my father continued, ignoring my nasty tone. "But I do know that Ray Murphy comes from a long line of anti-Semites. A recent investment loss, handled by a Jewish stockbroker, rekindled his dormant anti-Semitism. He also talked about his unsuccessful attempt to get into medical school and how his father had convinced him all the openings went to Jewish applicants with lots of money. Dental school was his second choice, and he was never happy with his profession.

"Kathleen Murphy doesn't appear to share her husband's prejudices. She seems like a decent woman. And, for years, Ray acted like a decent man. But this thing with Beth Levine stirred up emotions he couldn't control. His hate, which had just slid beneath the surface, came back and blinded him to everything except his anti-Semitism. He turned into a very sick man. It took a long time until the 'decent' Ray Murphy, if such a man does exist, came back onto the scene, but the guy I faced in court this week looked like that man. Now, he seems genuinely sorry he dragged his son into this mess, and he's admitted his guilt. That'll save us a long messy trial. I'm especially pleased that Brian will undergo counseling. He has a violent streak, and he needs a lot of help keeping it under control. He's got plenty of the bad Ray Murphy inside his brain. But he's certainly worth rehabilitating."

I shook my head and tried to smile. Part of me wanted to hug my dad and thank him for everything he was doing for the cause of law and justice, but the other part wanted to beg him to take a job selling ice cream. He leaned over and kissed my cheek before he left my room and headed for Temple Israel.

My mom, Sam, and I drove to the rally together. Rachel had said she'd meet me there. I figured Ricky would ask me to go with him, but he hadn't said a word about the rally when he saw me in school that day. I wasn't surprised. I mean, things had been pretty stiff between us for weeks. We talked a little, but we didn't exactly look each other in the eye. Every time I saw him, I wanted to stop and talk to him, but I couldn't. Things were different between us, and I wasn't sure there would ever be a way we could be friends again.

I couldn't believe how mobbed the temple was. Even though we'd gotten there fifteen minutes before the rally was to start, the entire temple parking lot was filled. A policeman rerouted us down a side street where both sides were filled with parked cars, but somehow we found a space. I couldn't imagine where the rest of the cars that kept pouring into the parking lot were going to park. Even though it was mid-May, it was a brutally cold night, and the three of us nearly froze to death walking the two blocks to the temple. The door of the temple was freshly painted, but I got a funny feeling when I looked at it. Like the ugly words were still there, just hidden behind the white paint. When we got inside the temple, it wasn't easy finding a seat. Luckily, my mother's friend had saved us three seats near the stage.

My father was standing on the stage, talking to a couple of priests. He didn't seem to notice the three of us. I looked around, but there were so many people I couldn't find Rachel. I wasn't thrilled about having to sit with my mother, but she looked so nervous I wasn't about to hassle her. Everything about this Murphy case still blew her out of shape. An example of how off the mark she was was the fact that she had let me drive to the temple, even though there was ice on the roads and I didn't have my permit with me. I just hoped I wasn't going to see a lot of my friends sitting together at the rally while I sat with my mother and brother.

As it turned out, I didn't end up sitting with my mother and brother after all. There were so many people without seats that my mother gave my seat to any elderly man who was standing at the end of our row. Seconds before the rally began, Rachel miraculously appeared at my side. She looked real nervous and grabbed my hand and held it tighter than she ever had before. "Hi, handsome," she said in a soft voice. "Am I ever glad to have found you." Before I could tell her how glad I was to have found her, the room grew eerily quiet. While Rachel and I huddled together against a wall, we watched Mr. and Mrs. Levy walk up to the stage where they took two seats among the long row of guest speakers. Actually, Mr. Levy was seated next to my father. Thoroughly confused, I glanced at Rachel. She offered me a weak smile and held my hand even more tightly.

My father was one of the first speakers. Introduced by the rabbi of Temple Israel as "our county's highly respected and outstanding district attorney," Dad delivered a great speech. "I promise to use all the talent and expertise available in my office to prosecute any hate crime perpetrators to the full extent of the law,'' he told the audience. ''No citizen of our country need fear the ugliness of prejudice nor the crimes it spawns. Our temples, churches, and schools must teach lessons of tolerance and fairness, and the law of this land must protect the values those lessons teach. It is the perpetrators of these crimes who need beware, not those who are targeted because of their religion, race, or ethnic origin.''

It wasn't just his words that had such power, it was his delivery. I had taken a speech course last year and I understand how important the delivery of a speech can be. My father's voice was strong and unwavering, and he maintained eye contact with every section of his audience. I glanced around at his audience during his five-minute speech, and I saw that everyone was listening intently to him. My mother was practically glowing. I also noticed that this audience was not just Jewish. I recognized several teachers from school who were not Jewish, as well as lots of non-Jewish kids and their parents. I was proud that they were all listening to the man who was not just the district attorney of Essex County but also my father.

After my father spoke, two ministers and one priest spoke, each one condemning the hate crime that would deface any house of worship. One minister was in tears as he spoke of his deep affection for the rabbi of Temple Israel and how deeply hurt both he and the rabbi were by this wanton act of intolerance. The other minister offered the rabbi a check from the members of his congregation to set up an interfaith council on tolerance. The priest spoke for only a few minutes and then surprised everyone by introducing Cardinal Sands of Boston who had come, unannounced, to address the group. I'd seen Cardinal Sands on television, but never in person. He was a tall, stately man, who looked even taller and more stately in his official garb—a long, silky, black robe lined and trimmed with red. The cross across the front of his robe was mammoth. What surprised me the most was the bright red yarmulke he wore on top of his thick white hair. I'd never noticed that when I'd seen him on television. The cardinal was an excellent speaker. He talked about brotherhood and tolerance and love and how important it was that the church not abandon the Jews today the way it had during other times of their difficult history. Those words were soothing and inspirational. If they were true, there would never be any reason for Jews to worry about prejudice and Holocausts.

Yet it was the final speaker of the day who had the strongest impact on the audience, and that was Mrs. Levy. Mr. and Mrs. Levy rose from their seats on the stage and walked to the microphone together, but it was Mrs. Levy's words which stunned the audience. Speaking so softly we all had to strain to hear her words, Mrs. Levy read three poems she had written and smuggled out of the concentration camp in which she had spent two years of her life. "I've never read them aloud before," she announced in her soft voice before she began to read them.

The first poem was about the "eyes which never stop watching and hating, glimpsing death and destruction all around, but never blinking, opening wide so they will not miss one glimmer of each atrocity." The second was about "a night so cold that all the fire in the world could not warm the blood of those who survive this night." Yet, it was the third poem that made the audience gasp, a poem about "a young girl with a naked head who wanders through the bodies, reading numbers that were names, touching thin cold arms, and making lists of those who died because Jews could no longer live; yet, she lived and wondered why and for how long, and if there would ever be a day when warm arms with numbers could tell a story no one would surely believe.''

I struggled to catch my breath as she read each painfully vivid word. I tried not to look at Rachel as her mother spoke, but I couldn't keep my eyes away from her face. The tears flowed down her cheeks. Never had she looked more beautiful, and vulnerable, than at that moment. I held her hand as tightly as I could, grateful that I was able to be there for her.

While the rabbi was offering his concluding remarks, I noticed Beth Levine for the first time. She was sitting in the first row, between her parents. She turned around at just that moment and our eyes met. If looks could kill, I would have died right on the spot. ''It's really *my* fault, this is all happening, you moron!'' I wanted to shout at her. ''*I* was the one who forbid you to date Brian Murphy, *I* made you break up with him, and *I* wrote the graffiti. *I* even created the concentration camps and killed six million Jews to make the world a safe place for Germans. Hate me, Beth. But that's not going to make the world a better place for you and me to live in.'' But I didn't say a word. I just stared back at her until finally she turned around and faced the stage again.

After the rally ended, my mother and Sam drove home together, and Rachel left with her parents. ''Your parents were unbelievable,'' I told her before she took off. ''Your mom blew me away with those poems. You should be so proud of her.''

''Oh, I am,'' she said. She was still holding my hand, but she'd lost her death grip the minute her mother sat down. ''But I'm just as proud of your father. He made me believe that maybe, someday, things just might be all right for all of us. I gotta tell you, I could just love that man.'' Then she leaned over and kissed me. ''But I already love his son,'' she said, and disappeared into the crowd to find her parents while I waited to go home with my dad.

The temple was nearly empty and I was helping the custodian put away the chairs while my father talked to a group of men when Ricky came over to me. "Your father was terrific," he said as he started to fold a few chairs himself. "Really terrific."

"Thanks," I said, and for the next ten minutes, the two of us worked together, silently stacking four huge piles of chairs. When we were through, I opened two chairs and we sat down beside one another.

"I've missed you, Zack," Ricky said, breaking the huge silence that seemed to have swallowed me up. "I'm real sorry for going after Rachel the way I did. I don't know what I was thinking."

"You were thinking that she was great looking and you'd like to be with her," I answered. "That was all."

"Yeah. That was all. I tried to nose in on my best friend's girlfriend. That was all."

Ricky looked so miserable I couldn't stand it. What was I trying to prove anyhow? The world was filled with people who hate someone who isn't the same color or religion and I'm hating the kid who's been my best friend since we were three years old. It didn't make any sense at all. "That's history," I said. "Can't we forget it already?" Ricky nodded, smiling broadly. "Hey, think I could snag a ride with you to school tomorrow morning?"

"I'll be there at seven-thirty," Ricky answered as he stood up to leave, and I knew that my best buddy would be honking his horn outside my front door at exactly 7:30 the next morning.

I was standing in the parking lot while my father talked inside to yet one more minister from Rockville when I saw Brian Murphy. He was wearing a hat, an oversized black woolen cap pulled halfway down his forehead, and a black overcoat with the collar turned way up. He also had dark glasses on, but I knew without question that it was Brian. He was walking quickly toward a car. I broke out into a jog and caught up with him just as he was pulling his keys out of his pocket. "I can't believe you had the guts to come here tonight," I said to him, "and to stay so late. How did you ever get the nerve to come to a rally held because of a crime you committed?"

"My mother made me," he answered.

"Oh, yeah, I forgot," I said. "You always do what your parents tell you to do, don't you? But I'm curious. Did you hear the poem from the woman who was a survivor? The one who talked about the numbers on peoples' arms? 'Cause I thought you might want to know that she was talking about herself. And the camp where that all happened was one of the camps whose name you wrote on the temple door. Isn't that an amazing coincidence?"

"Get off my case, man," Brian said, and he didn't look big at all to me. He just looked stupid in his black costume, stupid and frightened. And he had every right to be frightened. Every person who had come to this rally hated him for what he had done. Hated him for his hate crime.

I wanted to hate this kid so badly I could taste it. But the hate wouldn't come. He looked too pathetic to hate. And I was sick of all the hate. "You going to lacrosse camp this summer?" I asked him because I couldn't find the words to ask him all the other questions that were racing around inside my brain.

He looked surprised, but he answered me immediately. "I'm gonna try. I've got to check it out with the parole guy. How 'bout you?"

"Definitely."

"You guys had a great season this year. Except for your final game."

"Well, that's a different story," I said. Now that was a topic I'd love to throw around with the kid. But I saw the look on Brian's face. That subject was a no-go. The conversation was over. Brian turned and began to walk away from me. "Hey, Brian," I said before he got too far, "got one more minute?"

"I've got to get my car," he said. He was real anxious to get away from me, but that made me more determined to hold him there.

"It'll just take a second," I insisted. "I'll follow you to your car."

Brian shrugged, looked like he wished I would disappear, and led the way to his car. "Listen," he said, as soon as we reached his car, "I really gotta get out of here."

"I understand," I said. "I'll make it brief. It's just that I've been having sort of a hard time since that Worcester game."

"Hey, man," he interrupted me. "I had nothing to do with that hit."

"Your friend Beth warned me someone'd be aiming for me. I'm not blaming you. I just need to know how he got there in the first place. I mean, did you ask him to take me out? Is he a buddy of yours? Don't worry. You're not going to get into any trouble over it. It's history. I just need to know."

Brian took a deep breath and gave me a disgusted look. "Look, I don't want to get into this discussion," he said. "I'm on probation and I'm not about to take any risks with that. But I'll tell you he's part of a group of skinheads. He knew about your dad and you and me and he wanted to make a point. I didn't tell him what to do."

"No, but, you must have been glad it happened."

Brian shrugged. "I'm not as crazy as that guy," he said.

"Maybe not," I said, "but you're not exactly crazy about Jewish people, are you?"

"Listen, my case is over," he said.

He was getting angry, but I wasn't afraid of him. I might have been sitting on a different planet, but I didn't think he would lay a hand on me. Certainly not in the Temple Israel parking lot. Oh, he might get the gorilla to level me somewhere else, but he wouldn't get his hands dirty again.

"I'm out of here."

"Okay," I said. "But I sure would like to know when this hate thing is going to stop."

"Beats me," he answered. Mister Cool.

"I hear you're going to start a Holocaust course," I said. "Maybe that'll change the way you see things."

Brian leaned back against his car. Finally, he looked resigned to dealing with my questions. "I've already gone to one session. It was about history. With that Sonia Weitz lady—you know, the survivor."

"Oh, really? She's a great speaker. She spoke at our high school once."

"Yeah, well, she's not lecturing to a big group. It's just her and me."

"Oh, real intimate."

Brian sort of smiled. I wasn't sure if it was a smile or a smirk. I'd seen that look before—on his father's face. If I'd had to place money on the look, I would have bet on the smirk.

"You might call it that. She couldn't decide if I'm thoughtless or reacting to peer pressure. She's trying to get into my head."

Now it was my turn to smile or smirk. Mine was a smirk. "That must be pretty easy. I mean, there must be plenty of room in there."

Brian just stared at me. "I don't know about that. Our session was pretty boring. All she talked about were swastikas."

"Pretty evil things," I said.

"Guess so." He shrugged and looked at his watch. "Look, I really gotta go."

"I know," I said, "but just tell me this. Did your dad tell you all Jews were bad people?" I asked, anxious to hang on to him for one more second, to have my chance to get into this kid's brain. To see what made him tick. If I understood him, then maybe I'd understand all anti-Semites.

"Not exactly. He just didn't like them. Aren't there some people your dad doesn't like?"

I thought for a minute. "Just people who break the law," I answered.

Brian's face turned red. "Yeah, well, my dad thinks Jews make and break the law," he said. "That they control the press and the economy and the government. That they push themselves into places they aren't welcome. He says Jews are the reason everything's wrong in this country. And, face it, thanks to the Jews, he's losing his dental practice."

I shook my head. "You can't be stupid enough to believe that. He brought his problems on himself. He committed a crime."

"Yeah, well, he's paying for it. You know, my folks are splitting."

"I'm sorry," I said, although I wasn't. "And Beth—is she still your girl?"

He brightened a bit. "Guess you might say that."

"She's good-looking," I said as enthusiastically as I could manage.

Brian sort of smiled. "Yeah, she loves you, too," he said.

"I can't understand how you can like her so much and hate me," I said.

Brian shrugged. "Beats me, too."

"Well, she's better looking than me," I said.

"She didn't want that bozo from Worcester to take you out," he said. "She tried to get you not to play."

"Funny, I didn't see it that way," I said. "But I guess I'm too sensitive these days."

"Gotta go," Brian said. "See you on the lacrosse field." Then he opened his car door, slid into the driver's seat, and closed the door. He was through with me. Oh, we'd meet again on the lacrosse field this summer, but with our helmets fastened securely over our faces. And we'd give each other a good fight. On that field, we'd respect each other's playing abilities. It was just here, on the streets of the real world, that we couldn't seem to find the rules to play a fair game. Not just yet, anyhow.

Before I could say another word to Brian, a woman came over to the car. She was wearing a big fur hat that obscured a lot of her face, but still I could see the resemblance between this woman and her son. She was a lot smaller than her husband and her son. It had been so mobbed inside the building that I had not noticed them inside, but outside, in the freezing night air, I was here beside Mrs. Murphy and Brian.

Mrs. Murphy looked nervously at me and then glanced at her son. I didn't want to but I could feel this woman's pain. "I'm Zack Stone," I told her and she flinched. Then she shook her head back and forth.

"I'm sorry," she said softly. "We both are."

"I know," I said. Brian leaned over to unlock his mother's door without looking at me again. Mrs. Murphy reached over and touched my arm. I wanted to pull her hand off my arm, but I also wanted to touch it. Instead of doing either of those two things, I opened the passenger door and waited silently while she got into her seat. Then I closed the door and watched as Brian pulled out of the space and drove, way too fast, out of the parking lot.

When my father called my name, I was still standing in the same spot, staring at the space Brian's car had vacated. "Do you ever feel as if nothing makes sense, and no matter how hard you try to understand something, you will never be able to?" I asked my father when he walked over to me.

"All the time, Zack," he answered me. "But sometimes things seem clearer than at other times. Sometimes, there are answers. You just have to look extra hard to find them."

"Well, I'm not sure I've found the right answer yet. Even though Sam gave me a good one a while ago. Tell me, Dad. Do you think I should always keep my head down when someone aims a ball at me?"

"In the lacrosse net?"

"Anywhere."

My father thought for a minute. "Yes," he finally answered. "Keep your head down. But that doesn't mean your eyes are closed. It just means you're ready to grab the ball the second it hits the ground and throw it back into the midst of the opposing team—with every bit of strength you can muster."

"The rule book says that's okay, Dad," I said.

"Good," he said, "because I need to obey the rules."

"I understand," I said as we walked toward his car. And I did. I knew that Brian Murphy and the skinhead from Worcester weren't going to be the only two opposing players aiming at my head. But I was in this game to stay. Head down, eyes open, and grateful to every teammate who helped me keep the ball away from my net.